Journer

Journer

By
John P. Cock

transcribe books

Journer

Copyright © 2005 by John P. Cock

ISBN 0-9665090-5-6

Printed in the United States of America

Dedicated To . . .

Kaitlyn, Nolan, Lyndon,
Alex, Olivia, Marek, Christopher,
Hayden, Lauryn, Jack,
and all the little ones
on the great spirit journey,
who hopefully will read this book
when the time is right.

Other Books by the Author

Bending History:
Selected Talks of Joseph W. Mathews (2005);
co-editor; John L. Epps, general editor

At One With the Heart of Creation:
Reflections and Verse on the Spirit Journey (2004)
with Lynda Cock; foreword by Thomas Berry

Our Universal Spirit Journey:
Reflection and Verse for Creation's Sake (2002);
foreword by Thomas Berry

Motivation for the Great Work:
Forty Meaty Meditations for the Secular-Religious (2000); foreword by Thomas Berry

The Transparent Event:
Post-modern Christ Images (2nd ed., 2001);
comment by Bishop James K. Mathews

Called To Be:
A Spirit Odyssey (2nd ed., 2000); comments
by Wanda Urbanska and James Dodson

See online bookstores or e-mail
tranScribe-books@triad.rr.com
or visit web page or weblog
www.johnpcock.homestead.com
www.rejourney.blogspot.com

The world, Govinda, is not imperfect or slowly evolving along a long path to perfection. No, it is perfect at every moment; every sin already carries grace within it . . . – eternal life.

. . . Therefore, it seems to me that everything that exists is good – death as well as life, sin as well as holiness.

. . . I had to learn to love the world as it is, to love it and be glad to belong to it.

~Siddhartha, talking to his colleague about his spirit journey, in the little book by Hermann Hesse entitled **Siddhartha**

Called

When he was born his great-uncle looked at the shape of his head and declared he would be a preacher. His sister looked at baby brother and screamed. He weighed about eleven pounds, was long and very thin – skin stretched over bone. His family thought they would never fatten him up until they started feeding him Pet Milk and Karo Syrup. He survived and became a roly-poly with long blonde curls by the time he was two.

They named him Peter after his great-grandfather, a man with a long white beard, who definitely underwent a life-changing vision and calling, else he could not have been an elder in the Primitive Baptist tradition.

Peter spent his early years out in the country, as they say, and learned to explore and delight in his environment, reading the book of nature before he learned to read any other book. He was often seen bending over to kiss the flowers or talking to animals. At night he had to have his bed next to the window so he could revel at the universe as he said his prayers, with his eyes open.

He was not precocious but quick. He got

along well in school. He thrilled at being read to by teachers, or at home by his mother and older sister. He especially loved songs and poems. His first memorized poem was "Trees," the first few lines of which came back again and again throughout his life to remind him of the holy sanctuary of trees.

At church he looked forward to Wednesday night potluck dinners followed by Prayer Meeting, and Sundays when he spent hours at Sunday School, 11:00 service, choir practice, youth group, Sunday evening worship, and afterwards a couple of hours of fellowship at the Youth Center. The church became his second home.

He knew early on that he leaned toward things "spiritual," more than most of his peers. Everybody sensed it, his family, Sunday school teachers, ministers, youth directors, choir directors. All encouraged him to think about going into the ministry.

He went with his sister to a Sunday afternoon movie – a bit forbidden in that time and place – to see "A Man Called Peter," the story of the famous preacher Peter Marshall. His sister told him as they walked home that there would be another great preacher named Peter when he grew up.

A prominent industrialist, in the small mountain town they moved to when Peter was six, took him to visit the church-related college nearby where the industrialist was a member of the Board. Before Peter had graduated from high school, he was offered nearly a full scholarship to prepare for the ministry.

But, during his senior year in high school, Peter began to ask more hard religious questions than most folks cared to think about. He had begun to question myths in the bible: Adam and Eve and the snake, virgin birth, heaven and hell, walking on water, feeding the masses, and the other miracle stories of the New Testament.

His youth director saw such discussions as part of the natural process of religious maturation, so she encouraged them at the Youth Center, Sunday evening youth group, and retreats. Church adults began to buzz and told the minister that the Youth Center was raising agnostics, or worse. The preacher planned to fire the youth director, but forgot about it in the shuffle of being assigned to a new church. The new minister saw no problem as he came to the Youth Center to chat and fellowship with the youth. The agnostic rumor died down, especially as the youth began to help lead worship services on Wednesday and Sunday evenings.

Peter did his first preaching – really witnessing – that year, but stayed away from bible texts that he could not believe. He understood that what it meant to be a Christian was to try to figure out what Jesus would do in any given situation and then dare to do it, but he soon realized that this was not only hard to figure out but could get him into big trouble. What if he were to stand up in church and say the things he thought Jesus might say: namely, "This church is full of hypocrites, backsliders, pew-sitters, racists, middleclass, upright, and comfortable folks who have no intention of listening to and following me." Peter would not make a fool of himself by doing such a thing, so he let the radical Jesus notion go. But given his Christian idealism, he felt guilty and began to question his calling.

At college his freshman year, he and the rest of the class were rather afraid of their history professor, who could ask far more questions about life and faith than Peter had ever thought of. The professor seemed to delight in watching a pious and innocent student squirm. No one wanted to try to match wits with him and be intellectually humiliated. He just kept asking question after question, until one was without any rational defense for anything, from politics, personal morals, to religious beliefs.

"Peter, are you an American?"

"Yes, sir," Peter said, trying to act confident.

"How so?"

"Because I was born in the USA, sir."

"So birth is what makes you an American? Is that all?"

"No, sir."

"Well, what else makes you an American?"

"My beliefs."

"Which beliefs?"

"Believing in the Constitution."

"Name a belief in the Constitution you hold."

Peter thought hard: "That all men are created equal."

"Is that in the Constitution?"

"Yes, sir . . . I think so."

"Where does it say that in the Constitution?"

"Uh . . . I'm not sure, sir."

"What did Jefferson mean in 'The Declaration of Independence' by 'all men are created equal'?"

"That every person has equal rights."

"So women, poor folks, Negroes have equal rights with men in power?"

"Yes, sir. In the eyes of God."

"But do they have equal rights?"

"No, sir."

"Why not?"

When one was caught up in such public grilling, it seemed endless and without mercy.

Peter and the rest were getting the naïve stuffings beat out of them by the professor's Socratic methods. And because he kept attendance strictly, they did not miss class. They were learning the hard way to think things through, to think for themselves, not to just regurgitate a lot of facts on a test. His tests and exams were usually three big questions, that made the students sweat profusely, as if they were in dialogue with the professor as they struggled to write their answers. Peter sometimes got an "A-", allegedly the professor's highest grade.

Great rumblings were going on in Peter's religious life. He was finding out that he did not like to be around pious people, the ones who glibly said, "I'm praying for you," or "Just accept Jesus Christ into your heart." For such reasons he quit the pre-ministerial group on campus, called the "Holy Club" by many. One could even say the Holy Club ran Peter out of the ministry.

To earn needed extra money he took a job from a tobacco company to hand out cigarettes to any and all students. Peter and many of his closet friends became chain-smokers that year as they played Bridge and Hearts most nights till late, especially during exam week. Peter enjoyed being around his less pious friends. They seemed more authentic. He joined a fraternity of them and dated several from a similar minded sorority – but no one of them captured his heart.

On the matter of dating he had a philosophy: I am not going with any girl seriously who would not be a good candidate for a lifelong relationship. His dates were mostly to the indoor theaters. He had done the same kind of dating in high school, hung out with the gang, cruised Main Street, danced, went to the Dairy Bar, and just had fun. He was not into sitting in the backseat of a car with a girl at a drive-in theater. He almost lost control in just such a situation with a girl who was *not* a lifelong candidate. "No more of that!" he told himself. He was saving himself for someone special.

She showed up his sophomore year. He really fell for Suzanne and spent all his free time with her. She was Miss Right: good student, strong Christian, deep values, and a real beauty. His fraternity ran her for homecoming queen that spring. She lost by a vote because two of his fraternity brothers slept in. The poor guys were not easily forgiven.

He did not rush things but waited till the ninth date on campus when she finally reached over and kissed him as they sat on the sofa in the parlor of the women's dormitory. She took him home with her that spring and her parents approved of Peter right off. He visited her twice during the summer and brought her home the next fall to meet his family. All was a go. They were engaged at the fraternity banquet the next spring. Peter did have a pack of doubts, though. He almost got up the courage to call it off after the wedding date was set, but she was having the time of her life during the wedding preparation. And his parents loved her.

All else was going well. He graduated with a B.A. in English and was hired by a famous boys' school. So Peter had left the ministry before he ever got into it. But he and Suzanne did participate fully in a neighborhood church in the city and took leadership roles quickly.

Things were purring for the young couple. They were obviously meant to be and were doing well individually: Peter's several years teaching English at the boys' school, and being the obvious choice to be head of the department; Suzanne's becoming the lead teacher in the church's preschool.

About that time, Peter applied for a Ph.D. grant in English and got it. Their old college English professor and head of the department told them, when writing a letter of reference, that he was holding a place for Peter in the department when he had his degree in hand.

He and Suzanne loaded up their possessions in a U-Haul trailer and headed south to the university. Studying Old English and researching all the writings of Robert Browning became his grueling assignments.

Then, out of nowhere, Peter's life was changed, changed by a bullet in the head of his President. Somebody had assassinated one of his heroes.

From then on, the seemingly perfect couple was no more. Peter fell into several weeks of despair, knowing that teaching Browning's poetry would not deal with what had to be dealt with in his nation. He began to think of dropping the lucrative three-year grant and dismissing the teaching position that had been promised at his alma mater.

But Suzanne had bought that vision and would not easily give it up. She dreamed of being a professor's wife and raising a family on a small college campus. The line in the sand was about to be drawn.

Peter contacted his college president, who had become a denominational bishop. He advised Peter to enter seminary immediately: "You have only taken a meaningful detour, Peter, but now you have been called back to your calling."

Peter phoned home to tell his mother, but his father answered. When Peter told him his good news, his father said, "You're a fool if you let the Ph.D. scholarship and college job go."

Peter was definitely getting mixed signals about his calling.

Honest-to-God Despair

Peter easily registered for the winter term in seminary, also with a scholarship, but not as good as the one he had left. Suzanne's teaching enabled them to make it financially. A war was starting as they packed up and moved again, just four months after the last move. He said, without thinking, "Nothing waits when you're called." The word "called" was becoming her enemy.

Peter studied, went to class, and came home and studied. He was liking it too much, Suzanne observed. Her tales of her students fell on deaf ears. She taught, commuted, cooked, shopped, cleaned the apartment, did lesson plans and graded papers, and they saw very little of each other, though just a room apart most of the time. Peter became a recluse who seemed to study obsessively.

One night it erupted. Suzanne told Peter she despised his calling, his theologizing, having to type his boring papers that didn't make sense, and their having no life together any more. She finished her tirade with, "I am *not* going to be a minister's wife." After that, things grew more and more distant between

19

them. Their marriage stopped at her line in the sand, what she termed "*your* calling."

Soon Suzanne moved out and moved in with a cousin. Peter was stunned. He thought their love for each other would see them through. He could not seem to comprehend how his calling was dividing them. When he phoned her and begged her to come back and at least talk, she would ask him straight out, "Are you ready to leave the ministry, because that's not my calling?" Finally she told him to stop phoning, and if he did not, she would find a divorce lawyer. Since the assassination, their covenant until death appeared dead.

Peter's despair took him prisoner. He missed classes, stopped reading, started watching television till all hours, turned in his assignments late, and some not at all. He was on the way out if he couldn't catch hold. His faculty advisor had a few talks with him, but Peter's interest, courage, and energy to keep at his seminary courses were gone.

He was lucky, strangely, to be in his first course of pastoral counseling, which was not about books, lectures, or discussions. His first visit to the scary, gigantic city hospital to visit patients was hardly theoretical. His mentor figured that Peter could stand a shot of reality at least as real as what he was experiencing of late with his despair over his separation.

The mentor asked Peter to meet him at the hospital and they would do some visitations together. Peter did not know till they met that they would visit on the women's cancer ward. As they talked about the patients they would visit, Peter's mouth got so dry he could hardly swallow. He rubbed his perspiring hands on his khakis. What did he have to say to anyone in critical condition when he could not deal with his own life? The mentor sensed his trepidation and told Peter to observe the first visit before Peter would lead the conversations with two assigned patients.

They entered the room of an older black woman who was ill with bone cancer. The mentor asked how she was doing and she let loose.

"How'm I doin'? You damn well know how I'm doin', that I'm gonna die in this bed. So save your silly-assed questions for the next lady. Get out of here and let me alone!"

She turned her head and started to cry and then to heave a little. Peter wanted to run. What in God's name was he doing there?

The mentor, seemingly cool, said, as he tried to position himself better for her to see him, "Bessie, I'm sorry my question seemed silly. You know from our past conversations that I really care how you're doing, don't you?"

She didn't answer.

"Would you like to have some time alone and maybe I'll come by a little later?"

She kept crying and wiping her eyes and would not look at him.

He touched her shoulder and said, "Bessie, I'll see you later. God bless."

When they got outside her room, Peter grabbed the mentor's arm and said, "I can't do this."

The mentor looked at him eye-to-eye and asked, "What are you afraid of, Peter?"

"Of death and life and everything in between!" he retorted as he turned and hurried away without looking back. He didn't know where he was headed, but he walked extra fast, as it happened, toward a nearby park. He began to slow down after he saw the mentor was not behind him. A few deep breaths and a seat on a bench in the sun eventually slowed his heart rate.

He thought to himself, "I'm a basket case." After about fifteen minutes of the warmth of the sun and a beginning awareness of the breeze, and even the folks walking by, different reflections began to rise from somewhere.

"Peter, you are not a basket case. You are a young man who's been run into by a series of events in the past few months that have knocked you off your ass."

He almost laughed as he thought about St.

Paul sitting there in the dirt on the road to Damascus. Peter remembered reading a scholar who believed Paul hid out in despair for years before he turned around and took the *word* to the known world.

The voice said, "Peter, pick yourself up, dust yourself off, and walk to the bus. That woman up there with cancer is the basket case. She's inoperable. You're well. You have your whole life in front of you. Get up."

And Peter stood up and walked toward the bus stop. On the way he realized he was super hungry and ordered two hotdogs, with everything on them, and a Dr. Pepper. Did they ever taste good to him!

He was not miraculously healed, but he was back in his life, beginning to decide how he was going to live it again. He had a good conversation with his mentor and decided that he needed to go back and try some more visits at the hospital, if for no other reason than it had been therapeutic for him.

He asked how the second talk with Bessie had gone, only to hear that just before they had stopped by her room her doctor had told her she had a very short time to live, and to start thinking about what she and her family wanted to do in the time left. The mentor had failed to ask about her condition before they went in to see Bessie. Peter sighed.

After more visits to the hospital, he began to get the rhythm of three meals, classes, studying, and little to no television. He lay awake nights thinking of the assassination, of Suzanne, of visiting Bessie. One night he had a vivid dream of flying around with a bunch of angels, not knowing what he was supposed to do in particular as they swooped down and discharged their individual assignments. The dream ended before the revelation came, but he was refreshed by the thought of flying around caring for others rather than sitting around gazing at his own navel.

His theology class assignment was to write his credo, what he believed and how he came to believe it. He began to brainstorm his life experiences and was flooded by memories and images of his "profound life," he decided. He reflected on his readings in seminary so far, especially John Woolman's *Journal*, about a man's obedience to God that led to the Abolitionist Movement to free the slaves; and Dietrich Bonhoeffer's *The Cost of Discipleship* and *Letters and Papers from Prison*, the latter written before he was hanged by the Nazis for the failed attempt upon Hitler's life. Pretty clear examples, Peter thought, of what it meant to believe. He wrote,

Belief is a human's total dedication, not

blind and dutiful recitations of ancient creeds that were intellectually and politically cobbled at the early councils of the church. You can follow Jesus whether or not you understand the trinity or wonder what in the world the creeds are trying to get said with the "very God" and "very Man" language that bifurcates Jesus and staggers our God-given imagination. I believe Jesus was the son of God, and I believe I too am the son of God.

Peter was getting into it as he took his professor's credo instruction sheet seriously, "You can only believe what you believe, so be honest."

Peter respected Woolman and Bonhoeffer's theology all the more after reading of their lives. Those three little books were better than all the Barth and Bultmann and Tillich he had reflected on intellectually, even though those three theologians had fought battles against the Nazis in their own ways.

Peter was sniffing after the holy life, what it meant to be an honest-to-God Christian. Same question he was asking in high school. He wondered if the question would ever go away and where it came from anyway. He reckoned it was one of the strange arrows of the Holy Spirit. If so, he could write, and did, that he had experienced enough in his short life to believe in the Spirit of God, the Spirit of Jesus, and the Holy Spirit.

Another event would mark Peter's seminary journey. He relished knock-down conversations with fundamentalists after class and told them that they were in the way of Jesus' movement on earth now.

He found out that a group of them who believed in faith healing were going to meet in the chapel and heal one of Peter's friends who was stooped with paralysis from birth and could barely walk on his own with two special metal canes cupped to his arms. Peter charged into the chapel as they were laying their hands on his body and shouting their magic words.

Peter screamed with all his might, "You sons of Satan, get your hands off him!"

There was stunned silence as Peter rushed down the aisle and flung their arms away and helped his friend outside to a bench. They both were breathing extremely hard.

Peter said, "What in God's name were you doing in there? You wouldn't have been there against your will. Tell me!"

His friend said, as he tried to straighten his collar that was choking him, "Damn it, Peter! I was going along with it all the way, and then I was going to castigate them if nothing happened. It was all working out nicely until you ran in and went wild with your 'sons of Satan' scream. Where'd that mumbo-jumbo come from anyway?"

"Just something Jesus called the religious right of his time," Peter replied.

He seized the opportunity to write an article for the seminary journal that described the incident and released fierce controversy:

> I cannot think of anything more sacrilegious than this whole scene of would-be ministers of Jesus Christ doing a bunch of voodoo over the body of this great, deformed person. We are sent to proclaim freedom to all captives in Jesus' name, not to attempt to heal their physical bodies. Jesus' power is about allowing us to live the real lives we have – paralyzed or not – with a big "Y" for "Yes." That is faith. If the Gospel is about faith healing, the style demonstrated in the Chapel, then I'm out of here.

Peter graduated with honors. The Dean and others were very glad to see him go. His parents came, though it was obvious his father did not want to be there. Their communication had been forced since the fateful phone call about his calling, after which Peter shot off to seminary.

He had tried to contact Suzanne, but her

phone was out of order. She must have moved again. "Oh well," Peter brooded, "she would not have wanted to be there either."

Rev-run Journer

Peter stood in a church meeting room, before a committee of twenty-some ministers, to be approved for ordination. The head of the committee, an older, traditional minister, called the meeting to order. He nodded at Peter, but never called him by name.

"Sir, we just want to ask you a few questions. It won't take long. First of all, do you smoke?"

Peter was caught off guard. After a moment he answered, "Yes."

"Will you stop?"

"I haven't thought too much about it, no."

"Is that a 'no'?"

"For the time being, yes."

"Do you drink, sir?"

"Not much, just on special occasions."

"Will you stop?"

Peter began to feel abused by the questions, "For the time being, I think not. I mean 'no'."

"Maybe we need not go any further until we ask you to step outside while we discuss your answers thus far."

Peter replied quickly, "Before I go, may I ask you – the committee – a question?"

"I think you best go outside now, sir."

There was considerable shifting and grumbling from half the group of ministers, sort of in unison.

A single voice, "Let him ask his question."

The head of the committee cleared his throat and spoke again, but this time more agitated, "What is your question?"

Peter paused for a moment, then, with measured voice, said, "I was prepared to answer questions about the faith, about the deeper aspects of becoming a Christian minister, and the role of the church today. I am disappointed by the questions thus far . . . and wonder if you have more substantive ones?"

There was a buzz in the group of ministers. The chairman cleared his throat again.

"There seems to be a lot of disappointment here, sir. Maybe you need to go and reconsider what it means to be a minister in this denomination and come back at a later time."

There was louder grumbling among the ministers.

Peter spoke, "Sir, I am not trying to cause trouble, but I don't think I should be ordained a minister upon my answers to a couple of questions about petty personal morals. I hope this committee will discuss whether to grant me or refuse me ordination upon my written credo and the evaluation by others during my three years of seminary and related local church experience. I will be happy to respond to any questions about their comments in the folders before you."

The chairman, very red in the face, cleared his throat again, "Sir, we will call you back in a few minutes. And please do not smoke in the hall."

A mixture of laughs and boos were heard from the committee as Peter left the room.

Nearly thirty minutes passed, with obviously heated debate going on in the room. Peter paced the hall, going to the restroom, going outside to smoke. He had no idea that he would encounter such trouble with the committee, except maybe on matters of theology. Why hadn't someone warned him?

A committee minister came out of the room and spoke quietly to Peter.

"Peter, will you come back in, please?" He shook his hand and patted Peter on the back. "By the way, that was courageous what you did in there. Thank you for taking him on. He's a righteous . . . so-and-so."

The head of the committee called for order.

"Sir, it is with much reservation that we – I – extend to you the right hand of Christian fellowship." With an afterthought, he added, "The Bishop speaks highly of you, I've been told."

He came around the desk to shake Peter's hand, but did not look him in the eye. Peter graciously shook his hand. There was applause from a few more than half the ministers.

Weeks later, Peter was informed that he had been assigned his first church. He couldn't wait. He arrived in the mid-sized city in the southeast USA before he was expected. Wearing his new clerical collar and grey shirt he breathed deeply as he surveyed the dilapidated downtown church.

An elderly black lady with a rusted grocery store cart stopped him. She was thin, stooped, leaning on her cart, with her walking stick dangling from it. She wore a too-big dress with a gaudy broach, a black hat cocked to one side with a plastic flower stuck in it, and carried a black purse on her arm.

Peter stopped to tip his cap, "How are you today, M'am?"

"I's just fine, but this ole body I's walking around in has about had it. Hey, ain't you the new preacher here. My name's Mary. This is my beat, too, I want you to know."

Peter nodded in affirmation, "Glad to meet you, Mary. My name is Peter."

"Named after the 'Rock,' huh? Oh, I'll just call you 'Rev-run.' The last preacher always gave me a dollar when he see'd me. I's hoping you'd do at least dat much."

Peter was caught off guard, "Well, Mary, you won't believe this, but all I have on me is . . . seventy-six cents." He held it out in his hand.

"Well, dat'll have to do, I reckon. You can make it up to me next time. And don't you worry none. I ain't gonna send nobody else to see you. . . . Guess we have ourselves a deal, huh, Rev-run?"

Peter was uncomfortable in the situation, but said, "Ms. Mary, you say what you mean and I like that. I'll try to keep a spare dollar bill on me, but let's don't plan to meet but about once a week. How's that?"

"My, my. This here next generation sho is tight. But all right. Now you preach it da way it is to dose folks, you hear – whatever color you have in dose pews. They need a cattle prod is what dey need. Yes-sir-ree. My, dey stingy folks."

She turned and limped off humming "In the Sweet By and By," putting Peter's contribution in her big black purse.

Within the month Peter was leading an informal study group in the home of a member.

The host said, "Don't you think that's sort of radical, that every member is a minister?"

Peter, "Not at all, and I'll do you one better: any of you should feel free to park in the space with the sign 'Minister' in the church parking lot. First-come-first-serve since we're all ministers."

An older white man spoke up, "That's a catchy sentence, 'every baptized member is a minister,' but organizations don't last without a certain pecking order."

Peter responded, "Do you think Jesus believed in a pecking order? If he did, maybe it was 'the last shall be first.'"

"Yes," the man said, "but without Constantine and the Roman Empire's endorsement of Christianity, and all those councils when they hammered out orthodoxy and organization, there probably wouldn't be a church today."

"Maybe it would still be a bunch of house churches meeting in people's homes as we're doing here tonight. Would we be better off?" asked Peter.

A white lady remarked, "This sure is more meaningful than most any meeting I've been to in a church building."

Peter asked, "So, do we really take Luther seriously? Do we believe in the priesthood of all believers? Or should we leave the real leadership roles in the church up to the clergy – all male, by the way – like the Roman Catholics would still have us do some 500 years after the Reformation?"

The host cajoled, "Reverend, you're going to get us all in trouble."

Later on in his first year at the church, Peter and other ministers were talking to a white, single mother about her broken water pipe. A local television camera, invited by the ministers, was running. In this neighborhood, the plight of the poor was being reported more and more.

Peter asked, "Are you saying, Mrs. Dalton, that your water bill is $127 for last month, after the main pipe burst?"

Holding the hand of her little boy and carrying her baby, she answered, "Yes sir. I called the City but they're scared to do anything about it, 'cause they know who the house belongs to, a Mr. Jones. I think he must be paying them under the table."

Peter said, "Mrs. Dalton, we trust this problem will be fixed immediately. We have been trying to get in touch with Mr. Jones. In case he is watching, we are asking him to do the right thing."

She replied, "You sure are asking for trouble, but we thank you for your help. My children and I are really on some hard times."

The next day, Peter was asked to meet with

the members of the pastor relations committee of his church. They met in the church parlor, which was badly in need of repair.

The chairman, a black businessman, spoke, "Now, Preacher, we think you were really out of line with that TV interview. Mr. Jones says he's taking legal action against you and those other ministers. That's going to reflect badly on our church for sure. We think you have gone to meddling rather than doing what you were sent here to do. What do you have to say for yourself?"

Peter looked at the members one at a time, then said, "When I saw that single mother holding her children in front of that broken water pipe, I began to rage at such injustice."

The chairman said, "Nevertheless, we want you to meet with Mr. Jones and work this thing out before it really gets out of hand."

"I will gladly meet with Mr. Jones on these conditions: that he formally apologizes to Mrs. Dalton and her family, that he pays her back water bills, and that he promises to fix that water pipe the very next day."

"You know he won't do that. You've got to be realistic. What if we have to take this up with your District Superintendent?"

"I've heard you already have," replied Peter.

There was a pause as the chairman looked

at his agenda notes and said, "We'd hate to lose you, Preacher. The folks here think a whole lot of you. You'd do well to really pray over this and see to it that things get straightened out right away."

An elderly white woman began to speak without recognition, "I saw that broken water pipe on TV. I was so sad for that poor lady and her children that I about cried. I don't know Mr. Jones personally, but I hear he has property all over the city and that he treats his tenets badly. I don't much care about what he thinks or what happens to him. I think the real question is what happens to that lady and her children. So, I for one will stand behind the Preacher, because he's right."

The chairman said quickly, before anyone else could speak, "I was going to suggest we take some sort of vote here tonight . . ." but before he could finish, a young black lawyer interrupted him.

"Excuse me, Mr. Chairman. I was wondering if we might forego any vote and we *all* go pray over this, not only the Reverend. I really listened to what the previous speaker had to say. You know, it's hard to figure out the will of God, and usually it takes great courage to do it once you think you've figured it out. If I had to vote right now, I would have to stand with the Reverend along with the last speaker."

The chairman, about to lose his composure, said, "Sounds to me like you two have already voted. . . . Now, I'm willing to let this pass for the time being. I just hope the church doesn't lose members over it. Anybody else got anything to say before I ask the Preacher to dismiss us?"

No one else spoke. The consensus was strong. Peter dismissed the meeting with prayer. He waited to hear from Mr. Jones but never did, directly. The news on TV the next evening showed the water pipe being repaired by plumbers before a crowd of spectators. The problem was being fixed.

Two weeks later, Peter was asked to preach at Jesus' Tabernacle in the heart of the black section of the city. He was surprised when he saw Mary, the lady who greeted him that first day in front of his church. She looked like a different person in her big white hat, white suit, shoes, hose, gloves, bag, and white walking cane – white everything. She was as sassy as ever as she welcomed Peter.

"How you think you got invited to dis church, Rev-run? I happen to be a somebody here and I told dem you was a good man and to git you over here to see if you could preach as well as you talk on TV. That was a good thing you done for that poor mother and her babies."

Peter bowed to her and took her hand and held it, "Ms. Mary, you are one outstanding human being. I'm glad we're friends. And you look like a queen."

"Jus 'cause I's dressed up like dis ain't no reason you stop giving me my weekly contribution. You hear? God knows, I need ev'ry penny I can git my hands on. Now, you're lucky I's going to introduce you dis morning. You jus follow me."

As she headed up the aisle, everyone said, "Good morning, Miss Mary." When they got to the podium, she took Peter's arm and slowly mounted the steps and then sat in the first big chair. She motioned for Peter to sit in the chair next to her.

When the time came to introduce Peter, she got up slowly and ambled to the pulpit. She looked out over the packed congregation until everything was hushed. Then she began.

"I's been knowing the Rev-run here ever since he come to town. I know'd when I first saw him he was God's man. You can tell such things if you're right with the Lord ya'self. Then you all saw him on TV. He made us followers of Jesus proud when he helped dat poor family with da big water bill."

There were many shouts of "Amen!" and

"Praise the Lord!" followed by a standing ovation of applause. Peter was not used to such as this in his services. He nodded his head, embarrassed.

Mary went on, "We all knows about Journer Truth, how she was not afraid to do and say God's truth (shouts). Rev-run Peter, here, he's the same stock as Journer Truth, jus a different color and sex (laughter and shouts). I think we ought to give him a new name dis morning. We could call him Journer Justice (shouts). We could call him Journer Peter . . . but dat don't sound right (laughter and clapping). Let's jus call him 'Journer,' 'cause that's all any of us is."

She looked at Peter, "You, Rev-run, is somethin' special. You been sent here to show us how to journey. That's right (shouts). You be on the great spirit journey of our Lord (shouts and clapping), the great journey without end (more shouts and clapping). We'll call you Journer (all standing and clapping)!"

Mary slowly made her way back to her chair. Peter stood in place till she walked by. He said, "God bless you, Ms. Mary. These people love you."

She replied, "Now, don't you embarrass me with your preachin'."

He did not. He read his text from the 14th chapter of the Gospel of Matthew:

When the disciples caught sight of . . . [Jesus] walking on the water they were terrified. "It's a ghost!" they said, and screamed with fear. But at once Jesus spoke to them. "It's all right! It's . . . [just me], don't be afraid!"

"Lord, Lord, if it's really you," said Peter, "tell me to come to you on the water."

"Come on then," replied Jesus.

Peter stepped down from the boat and did walk on the water, making for Jesus. But when he saw the fury of the wind he panicked and began to sink, calling out, "Lord save me!" At once Jesus reached out his hand and caught him, saying, "You little-faith! What made you lose your nerve like that?"

Using the text, Peter illustrated times of his own strong faith, when we could walk on water, metaphorically, as the disciple Peter did in the story. But then waves came at him and he took his eyes off Jesus and began to sink.

"Over and over this happens to each of us on the spirit journey – remembering we are all 'journers,' as Ms. Mary said so well. We all end up begging for help when we are about to sink, which means we are still people of faith – but what Jesus called 'little faith,' meaning we are weaker in our faith than before, but we are still persons of faith, still on the journey (shouts).

"Always Jesus goes on before and hollers back, 'Peter, come on out on the water again. Trust me.' Jesus says, 'Step on out, Peter' (shouts).

Mary shouted, "Amen, Journer. Preach!"

Peter was lifted up by the congregation's spirit. "That's the journey we're all on. Jesus never stops saying, 'Step on out (shouts). Fear not (shouts). Pick up your little-faith and step out here with me (more shouts). I'll catch you if you fall. . . . Step on out'" (clapping begins).

A few in the congregation started the chant, "Step on out," and everybody picked it up. It took on a life of its own, "Step on out." They were standing now, and every time they said "step," they began to put the right foot out. Each pew looked like a chorus line. The organ cranked up. The choir swayed and led the chant, "And Jesus said," and the congregation responded, "Step on out."

Over and over the chant and dance went on. Mary reached out and tapped Peter's arm with her white cane. He had not finished his sermon, but looked at Mary, nodded, and went back and stood at his seat and joined in the chant and dance, awkwardly, "Step on out."

Peter sensed he could walk on water again.

Church Reformer

Peter spent several years in his first congregation, especially focusing on social injustice and trying everything he could think of to take his people with him out on the front lines. But it seldom happened. They admired him but left him out there by himself, mostly. He always corrected his members when they said the church *has* a mission. He would not be satisfied until the church understood itself *as* mission. He was lonely and tired, and a little singed – but not burned-out.

He had thought about Suzanne daily but had lost contact with her. Her cousin told him to let her go. He was afraid to launch an all-out search for fear she *would* contact a lawyer. Yet, he was remaining true to his covenant until it was dissolved, one way or another. He held out hope as long as he had received no divorce papers.

Wide open to ways to catalyze his congregation, Peter read an article in *Time* magazine about an ecumenical group working in the ghetto on the West Side of Chicago. What really fascinated him was their common life-style to sustain themselves in mission as they lived in a deserted seminary. It reminded him of Bonhoeffer's book *Life Together*. He clipped the article.

A few months later a minister friend informed Peter of a seminar for local church leaders and ministers that he had registered to attend. Peter read the brochure and immediately realized the seminar leaders were members of the ecumenical group he had read about in *Time*. He recruited three of his lay leaders to attend with him.

Peter could tell from the beginning that this was going to be a different type of seminar. The first half was a reintroduction, for him, to 20th century theology; the second half, building models to implement in the local parish and congregation. Would it be too heavy, too demanding, for his laypeople? He reminded himself they were adults.

The first session began with a talk on the theological revolution of the 20th century. The first paper was an excerpt from Rudolph Bultmann's essay on "The Crisis of Faith," lifting up times when the "question of God" is raised. The "mysterious power" that drives humans into life and cuts them off Bultmann calls "God," and a person's relationship to that *power* makes all the difference.

The two seminar leaders were very particular with language as they kept pushing for life examples. One could not get away with the words "God," "Christ," "Holy Spirit," and "Church" without "grounding" them. Most church persons, they maintained, did not know what they meant by churchy jargon that kept second-story, other-worldly images of faith alive and did not sustain them in their daily living.

Peter found himself wanting to say "Amen" many times. The leaders said Bultmann is very clear. The question before the seminar: Is his image of God true or not? The answer one gave indicated his or her own image of God. It was obvious that the seminar sought to clarify the participants' foundational life assumptions, and then whether they seemed adequate. If not, change – which of course most fight to the death to keep from doing.

During the second session, the "Happening of Grace" or the "Christ Event," the leaders offended some participants as they illustrated personal life events that popped the balloons of their illusory assumptions, what one called "holy lies." Everyone knew that being confronted with raw truth by one's spouse could be a life-changing event, but few wanted to associate such a happening with the Christ they knew from Sunday school.

With the Christ event came the gracious

word that "all is good," "my life is received," "the past is approved," and "the future is open." Drawn graphically in an "X" on the board was the *word* that changes lives, if one embraces it or says "yes" to it. The leaders inferred that the *event/word* was part of the very structure of life, that it happened to every human – sometimes quite forcefully, as with Paul – and that the church came along and named such a profound life-changing event "the Jesus Christ event."

After studying Paul Tillich's sermon "You Are Accepted," there was much debate over what is "sin" and what is not. Tillich named sin the life dynamic of "separation" from self, others, and the ground of being.

Then came Tillich's grace happening paragraph. The leaders asked, "When has grace happened to you?" The participants were deeply addressed by the realization that grace had happened to them over and over, in big ways and small, and that they were indeed accepted just as they were – separated, broken, sinful, full of illusions. It sounded and felt so revelatory, but upon further reflection Peter saw it as the same gospel he had heard before, only in contemporary terms that made sense. During that session on grace, Peter observed that one of his laypersons was crying.

The third session, "Freedom: The Life-style of the Holy Spirit," started with a talk on the roles a person of freedom plays. Peter wrote down the quote, "The situation is never your problem." He was addressed by numerous human examples of the style of freedom that finally answers to no authority.

Then they tackled an excerpt from Dietrich Bonhoeffer's *Ethics*, on "Freedom," the book he was writing in prison right before he was hanged, naked, by the Nazis.

During the dialogue they were confronted with the truth that if one is 100 percent free and 100 percent obligated, he or she is a truly responsible person: absolutely obligated to everyone and absolutely free from the authority of anyone or anything, even the authority of one's religion. Every decision is to be made in the crucible of deciding for oneself what is "the will of God" and then doing it with "open eyes and a joyous heart."

Peter floated out of that session and back to his room. He was giddy about, yet fearful of, the freedom he realized he had. He was filled with possibility as he knew big life decisions could be demanded at any moment. He began to see he could go anywhere, do anything. All it took was a free decision – as if there was any other kind of decision. His internal dialogue was going full throttle, so he took a quick walk and a shower.

The group needed a break and looked forward to an evening of art: Picasso's "Guernica" and the award-winning movie "Requiem for a Heavyweight," with Anthony Quinn, Mickey Rooney, and Jackie Gleason. But it was not a light evening, either the Picasso conversation or the movie, with the long conversation afterwards. The participants were having a test on the seminar thus far: "In the movie, where did you see the activity of 'God'? the 'Christ event'? the freedom style of the 'Holy Spirit'?"

Peter thought to himself this is not even a religious movie. The leaders said it is a piece of life and is therefore as religious as any other piece of life. During the group reflection they came to realize that Miss Grace Miller, in the movie, a social worker out to do good in her way, would have deprived freedom from the main character she was out to "save." Even a mobster delivered the freeing *word*, paradoxically, to bring new life to the punch-drunk heavyweight fighter.

The seminar was saying that the *mysterious power* was happening in every life. The participants' wrapped-up belief systems were coming unwrapped. They were learning the old-fashioned way as their personal dogmas were being called into question.

The next morning started with the "Church"

section. The talk was riveting: the *people of God* and *God's people* are both loved equally by God, but the former give themselves on behalf of the latter. They heard a roll call of those in history who had decided to be the church – some without ever going to church or professing faith – even sacrificed to be the church, and what difference it had made.

Next they studied H. Richard Niebuhr's short paper called "The Church as Social Pioneer." They discussed what the church is *not* and *is*, and that it has nothing to do with the institutional building on the corner called "church" – in the first instance. Niebuhr was talking dynamics: when you see this, this, or this going on, that is what I point to with the word "church." He wrote that the church always acts "on behalf of" the other, not itself. The body of Christ "reduplicates the deed of Christ." The body of Christ "has faith in God," as Jesus did, which was radical faith. The air was very rare after that session. Most participants were under judgment. Were their churches being the church? Was each of them being the church? Was it possible today? It had to be. Decision, decision.

Peter wrote in his journal that night his summary of the seminar thus far:

When something radical, total, and un-
conditional is demanded of me, with awesome spirit I am experiencing God.

When something happens and announces
I am absolutely accepted and I accept that
fact, with grateful spirit I am experiencing
Christ.

When something releases me to be slave
to no thing and free for all, with swelling
spirit I am experiencing the Holy Spirit.

When I see and respond to creation's suf-
fering, with willing spirit I am being the
Church.

They had finished the first half of the
seminar and were drained spiritually and
physically. They were more than ready for the
practical, or so they thought.

During the next four sessions, the leaders
guided them through the most comprehensive
context and intensive planning process most
had ever experienced. They heard talks on
contextual ethics, the external mission of the
congregation, the internal dynamics of the local
congregation, and the global spirit movement.
They created a grid of the world, a global
problem analysis, a map of their local parishes,
their parish analysis and strategic objectives,

their congregational training plan and their local church cadre operational scheme. They had a plan in hand to go back and revolutionize the local church if they decided to implement it. A daunting consideration.

All that was left was the closing ritual and evaluation. They had participated in worship experimentation throughout the four days, looked at art forms, and had done conversations over meals. But the closing ritual was the high point. A leader took a loaf of bread and just tore it in two, saying, "This is the brokenness of life. We can take it into ourselves and feast upon it," and he did, passing it to the other leader to tear off a piece and eat. Then the first leader took a cup of water, poured some of it out on the table, and said, "This is the spilled-out-ness of life, and we drink it (which he did), knowing that our lives, spilled out as they are, are whole and accepted." Awe was thick in the room. The central ritual of the church came to life. Peter was transfixed.

During the evaluation, many shared that it felt like they had been together for a month, because they had experienced so much depth and made so many decisions about their congregations and parishes – and their own lives. Some got out their negative criticisms, but for every one mentioned, someone else turned it into a positive reflection on the seminar.

The leaders told about the work of their parish experiment in a Chicago ghetto and about their group, and how they were some two-hundred, clergy and lay families, who were experimenting with an ordered life-style together. They asked for financial support and told of the seminars that could be set up for church members and friends. A leader turned to a young black minister to send the group out, and as he was thinking about that, the leader addressed his life by telling him how strong a leader he could be, even another Moses, if he had the courage. Of course, the black minister had a hard time speaking after that.

The seminar was over, but Peter lingered. After chatting with his three lay leaders, who were shell-shocked and afraid of the implications of the seminar for themselves and their congregation, he caught up with the seminar leaders and asked them about their schedule, only to be invited to go with them to a restaurant and chat before their flight back to Chicago.

Peter immediately asked what training opportunities they had for him in Chicago. He was ready to learn all their methods in depth, because he saw great hope for the future of his church using such methods. When could he go?

One of the leaders recalled that Peter had

answered the meal conversation question – What would you want written on your tombstone? – with "church reformer."

"Peter, it's not about reforming your one little church. It's about reforming the church universal. It's about reforming all religions for the sake of the world. How many churches are there across the globe? Millions. Now, if you're interested in reforming the whole church, then you come tomorrow. Hell, you are absolutely free to march up to the airport counter and buy a ticket and fly back to Chicago with us. But if you're just interested in reforming your one little church, then I wouldn't even think about coming to Chicago."

Peter broke eye contact. His citadel had been penetrated. There was nowhere for the conversation to go from there. They awkwardly ate, got through their "thank-you's," hand shakes, and "hope-to-see-you-again-soon's," then went their separate ways.

Peter – "church reformer" – had some decisions to make.

Reunion in the Ghetto

Peter had been with the ecumenical group in the ghetto in Chicago – supposedly for training – for about three months and was frustrated enough to leave. He told himself the staff was too insensitive and too regimented. They rose at 5:30 every morning, rushed to corporate worship, sat through a breakfast collegium, ran to the day's assigned tasks, ate dinner together with an intentional conversation and study, and fell into bed, that is, if not assigned to wash dishes for a couple of hours or be a security guard of the property all night. He had lost weight, was sleepy and moody, and was not getting the kind of affirmation he'd always been used to. Besides, the ghetto was a wreck to look at in spite of all the work that had been done over several years.

Then the strangest thing happened. He saw her in the hall from a distance and slid around the corner, hoping she hadn't seen him. It was Suzanne!

What in the name of God was she doing there? He got his breath and decided he'd might as well get it over with and face her. As he walked toward her, she smiled and said,

"Hi, Peter," before he could say a word. They did touch hands for a moment before Peter let go awkwardly.

"What are you doing here?" he asked.

"I came to take the weekend seminar," Suzanne replied.

"Really? How did you hear about it?"

"I heard you were here and checked into this thing that brought you all the way up here away from your church. I was intrigued by the article I read in *Time* magazine and thought I'd take a look for myself."

"Yea, it was a good article. Which seminar are you taking?"

"The one on the theological revolution," she said.

"But I thought you were through with the church."

Suzanne replied, "That was just the traditional church, the one my husband left me for. Now that I see he's not a part of the traditional church at this time, and sort of acting like a layman, then I think he and I could find something in common." She smiled and looked straight at him until he turned away.

Peter did not know what to do. She was so direct and looked so beautiful to him, all aglow. He finally said, "Would you like to walk out in the courtyard?"

He kept avoiding her eyes. They got to the

cement wall around the chapel and sat down. His heart pounded.

"Where have you been living since we last made contact?" he asked.

"I've been in grad school in social studies. At State."

"What kind of courses?"

"Mostly those related to community development."

"Really?"

"Yes," she said, with a smile that he missed as he continued to look everywhere except at her.

"When do you finish?"

"I just did," she said.

"So what next?"

"I'm looking around. Who knows, I might stay on here a while and see how I can help."

Peter swallowed and let out a big breath.

"Are you okay?" she asked.

"Who, me? Yea, I'm fine, but seeing you here is unbelievable. I'm at a loss for what to say."

"Why don't you take the seminar with me, that is, if you can. Then we will have something to talk about."

"Good idea. I'll see if I can change my assignment. Sure. Great idea. Sit here and I'll be right back."

He ran off like a kid. In a few minutes he

returned to say it would work out.

"Want to come up and see my room?" just popped out of his mouth. He felt odd asking this strange lady – his wife – to do such a thing.

"Sure," Suzanne said.

On the third floor of the dilapidated main building, he opened the door to a very small room, about 12' by 14', with meager furnishings, but everything seemed in its proper place.

Peter said, "This is not much, but I've been sort of monking it since . . . we separated. I guess you would say austerity is good for the soul." He chuckled nervously.

"Who sleeps on the upper bunk?" she asked, as though not listening to his last remark.

Nonplused, Peter answered, "Nobody."

"You think it would be all right if I roomed with you this weekend?"

Peter's mouth gaped open. He swallowed again. "Sure, if you think you'd be comfortable up there."

Suzanne said, "If I'm not, I'll jump down and sleep with you."

Peter about exploded. What is going on here? Who is this woman in my room? She looks exactly like my wife used to look, but. . . .

He finally said, "Well, it's about time to go sign up for the seminar. It's always good to go early and get a good seat. Do you want to sit together?"

"No," she said, "I want to sit across the table from you and look at you all through the weekend."

"Well, let's go," said Peter, who stumbled and about lost his balance as he reached for the door.

"After you." He looked her up and down as she walked through the door ahead of him. Wow, he thought, she looks better than I remember. What am I getting myself into? He wanted to reach out and hug her to him and never let her go. But he told himself to be very cool and not to blow this weekend, not after all this time. Be cool.

The seminar opened with the God section and went on until about 10:00 that evening. Peter hardly heard a word as he tried to figure out all the inconspicuous ways he could look at Suzanne across the table. She caught him looking at her several times and melted him with her smile. He knew again like for the first time why he was so attracted to her. She was a woman of beauty, style, grace – *anima* – and now, seemingly, a commitment to service like his, which he'd never really seen in her before. If she dug the seminar as he did the first time, watch out, world. Watch out, Peter. He had this feeling that the second time around may be for keeps.

They didn't stand around after the seminar but wound their way toward Peter's room. He showed her the women's restroom down the hall and reminded her they had a sink in his room, one of its few amenities.

He was fidgeting around when she tapped on the door and walked in after his "Come in."

"That was a cold shower, Peter," she said, as she shivered.

"I'm so sorry, but be glad you had water pressure. It comes and goes."

She draped her jeans and shirt over the chair after she saw there was no other place to put them.

She looked at his decor around the room and his quotes on the wall. She took her time but said nothing. She was circling his space, settling in. Peter was tense.

"Would you like a glass of wine? It's warm, but you used to like it that way."

"Of course."

He poured and gave her a regular water glass half full.

She said, "Let's drink a toast."

Peter, "To what?"

Suzanne, "To the great journey we've been on together . . . and apart."

They drank and made lingering eye contact.

Peter, "Let's drink to this reunion."

Suzanne, "Let's drink to this night."

Peter gulped his wine down.

She put down her glass and moved close to him. He just stood there, with his glass in his hand. She took it and placed it on the table beside hers. She then pulled off the robe he'd loaned her and threw it over the chair, on top of her other clothes. She wore a short, thin, white, knit gown and stunned him as she reached to turn off the overhead light, pulled the curtains open to let in some street light, and then moved right up against him. Peter was experiencing "The Rapture" that he thought he didn't believe in. She lifted her hands up to his face and stood on tiptoe as she tenderly kissed him. His lips quivered. He finally put his arms around her waist and leaned back and beheld her radiance, and her luscious body.

She said, "Peter, do we have any music?"

He fumbled as he reached for the radio and turned to an FM station, which was playing

. . . When somebody needs you
It's no good unless he needs you
All the way
Through the good and lean years
And for all the in-between years
Come what may

Who knows where the road may take us
Only a fool would say
But if you'll let me love you
It's for sure I'm gonna love you
All the way
All the way

Both knew they were playing their song.

They danced so very slowly, in place, and tender kisses turned to passionate ones. The dam of the years apart broke. Deep union was the order of the night as they lay together and made love on the lower bunk, until they threw the mattress on the floor because of the noisy springs. Never had they given themselves so fully to each other.

It seemed that they'd just gone to sleep when they woke to the sound of the gong on the hall and the stentorian voice of "Praise the Lord, Christ is risen," to which Peter responded through a yawn, "He is risen indeed."

Suzanne, with exclamation, "What was all that?"

"Oh, that's the morning wake-up ritual."

"Oh," she said. Then she tenderly kissed her first and only husband good morning as she ran her hand through his mussed-up hair. She rubbed his shoulder as she paraphrased Bultmann from the God session the night before, "That 'mysterious power' drove us to love last night, huh, Peter?"

He sighed, "Yea," and he looked straight into her lovely eyes and then held her, and held her tighter, making sure all this was real and praying they would never leave each other again.

Parish Demonstration

After a month, Peter and Suzanne decided that they wanted to stay awhile and participate fully in the parish demonstration project on behalf of churches everywhere. Peter remembered well the words of his pedagogue after the course for clergy and lay that brought him to Chicago: "If you're interested in reforming the whole church, then come. But if you're just interested in reforming your one little church, then don't even think about coming to Chicago."

When Peter told Suzanne what the seminar leader had said, she threw back her head and laughed. She said, "Wow! He knew where your heart and kingdom were. These people have a way of grabbing the juggler vein and squeezing it till you say 'uncle.'"

Peter added, "Or till you say 'I will.'"

They sat in silence for awhile before Peter came up with the quote of the day: "If God wants us to stay on here, then he'd better let us know."

Suzanne chided him. "Yes, God, take all the ambiguity out of it and just tell us your will for our lives, this very moment. Peter, do you think that was what Bonhoeffer said when he was trying to decide whether to leave the New York seminary professorship and go back to Germany to be with his people during the war? Do you think that's what Bonhoeffer said when he was trying to decide whether to join the plot to assassinate Hitler? No, he said in his 'Freedom' paper we've been studying, 'Observe, judge, weigh up, decide, and act.' And remember the words from the song: 'To no principle, no law, to no authority can you withdraw. You decide it all alone.' So come off your telling God to tell us what to do. We've got to figure out and decide what God wants us to do, then do it. And for the umpteenth time, God is not a 'he.'"

Peter could not believe it. Before him stood the woman who left him because he was trying his heart out to be the church and do the will of God. Now she is telling him what it means to do both. He was definitely humiliated – and grateful – to have such a partner at this juncture of life.

He finally looked her straight in the eye and said, "Okay, lady, you asked for it. Let's fish out in the deep water. Either we go all the way with this mission on behalf of the whole church, all religions, and the future of mankind, or we go back where we came from and figure out something else to do. We can leave our old life-style behind and turn a deaf ear to our families and friends when they tell us we are fools. And believe me, they will. Wait till we start selling our books, our furniture, our cars, and skinny down to a few suitcases. This *is* very nuts in the eyes of the world. You know that, don't you?"

The temperature in the room had risen several degrees. Their eyes were glazing over. To say they were awed by the decision they were making was the literal truth.

Suzanne came over, took his hand, and led him to the lower bunk bed. They lay down and held each other tightly and lovingly until their racing hearts and breathing slowed down and got in sync. They softly sang more of the little song that came out of Bonhoeffer's "Freedom" paper, to the tune of the Beatles' "Yellow Submarine."

Refrain:
Free men live in responsibility,
    duty bound and free in relativity;
Free men live in responsibility,
    whoever they may be, their deeds are history.

Last stanza:
Obligation is the call;
    to God and neighbor surrender all.
The free venture is the deed
    rendered up to meet the need.

Again they sang the refrain, then hummed it until they began to kiss. They made tender love and fell into a blissful nap.

When they woke, Peter began to spin on what was going on earlier in their deciding. "Decision can join us to God by awakening us to his presence, don't you think? It's sort of like decision is the bridge between the temporal and the eternal. Or decision is a break between the old and the new, that is, if it's a big decision like we're making."

Suzanne squeezed his hand tightly. "You know, you're my kind of theologian." She paused, then added, "I just wish one little thing."

"What's that?"

"Please stop calling God 'him.' And the 'Responsibility' song we were singing, what can we say to change 'free men' to include us women?" Then she tickled him, pecked him on the lips, and jumped up and did a few moves of the Twist, which she'd hardly done since high school dances. For her finale, with her arms stretched above her head, she shouted, "Freedom is awesome!"

She declared their consensus in the form of a question, as she put on a silly smile, "Peter, so you think we have made the decision to stay and throw ourselves into the 'breach of history,' as they say in the church section of the course?"

He said without hesitation, "I do. Don't you?"

She said, "I do. . . . Sounds just like our wedding vows, 'I do' and 'I do.' It's at least that serious a decision, don't you think?"

Peter, with a twinkle in his eye, said, "I do."

Then he tickled her back. They gave each other a big hug, freshened up, walked hand in hand a couple of blocks to the elevated train stop down on Homan, and road to the Loop to celebrate their big decision to stay – only God knew how long – with a Chicago pizza and a pitcher of beer.

Peter was assigned to help create a blocks network where he and a community leader went door to door and began to find out who was the symbolic leader on each block. He then began to chat with them about their accomplishments and vision for their blocks. Trust was key. Next they brought the block leaders together.

It was slow going, but he began to see their southern black passion – many had migrated from Mississippi – through what they said. He and Suzanne got several invites to eat barbecue and play Whist. There was real spirit and camaraderie at such events.

The block leaders' first cooperative project was a spring clean up for the forty-block area, or what the ecumenical group called a "parish." Only about six blocks had some participation, but it was a start. It began to happen. They decided to have a couple of demonstration blocks to attract the attention of others. Individual block participation was easier to catalyze.

Suzanne worked with the community symbol guild. Before she arrived, their big project had been the creation of a fourteen-foot-high Iron Man of black, rusting iron, a skeletal structure of a figure with hands reaching to the sky. Welded from the beams of buildings burned during the riots, it held the image from Jeremiah, "I will make you a pillar of iron who will stand." It stood tall in the community plaza. The preschool had red t-shirts with the Iron Man on them for their uniform. They understood as they reached up like the Iron Man in one of their rituals. Talk about a master symbol of the community – t-shirts, a comic book, murals, buttons, songs, stories, rituals – all about the Iron Man.

Suzanne was assigned to help design a really classy booklet about the community that they could give to visitors, funding sources, and government agencies. It was to be a slick red cover with a black graphic of the Iron Man. Inside, pictures and text especially focused on existing and projected projects in housing, the small shopping center, the auto service center, the jobs training and placement center, the infant school, the preschool, the afterschool program, the elders center, the health clinic, the blocks association, and the safe streets program – which catalyzed established male participation. Several of these programs were housed in the community center, which was an old union hall.

The booklet took months, especially since the team had to raise its own money to publish it. One Chicago celebrity born in the community was the major benefactor of the booklet. Her first cousin, from the community, and Suzanne made the call to her office in the Loop and were told to do it right and she'd pay half the cost. Leaders of the community along with the ecumenical staff used it soon after publication to give out as they spoke in Washington at a Congressional hearing on inner-city programs that work. They were becoming a demonstration parish for sure, even though most of the community would not have called it that.

Peter and Suzanne were traipsing around the community as if it were a cakewalk until one evening one of their white staff members was dragged into an alley and raped. She later was taken back home for extended mental care. Not long after that, Suzanne was walking in the community with two other white staff when a black youth with a stocking over his head ran by and cut her shoulder strap with a switchblade and snatched her purse without slowing down. Till she died she would have the two-inch scar on her arm to remind her of that event.

Reality set in: they were living in a 98 percent black ghetto on the West Side with the highest crime rate in Chicago, where poverty and welfare cases were the norm, where killings and beatings often took place, where drug dealers, drunks, gangs, and prostitutes were common. And this was a community where many buildings were burned during the 1968 riots and their white staff were marched out of their buildings at gunpoint by the outside gangs – but fortunately they were not harmed because people of the community pleaded for their safety. Peter and Suzanne had been naïve, liberal do-gooders up to that point in their ghetto experience. They had heard the gruesome stories but considered themselves invulnerable. Now their faith could become more authentic as a pinch – no, a good dose – of fear set in.

And Peter was dealing with a whole lot more: a "new" wife, who threatened his maleness with her newfound selfhood, called his male chauvinism and patriarchal theology into question, and intended to be equal in every way – even a little more than equal it seemed to him at times. Added to all that was his new role of serving in a situation where he was no longer the leader. His life was definitely undergoing great change as he strove to do God's will.

Child of God

Not since the assassination of his President or not since Suzanne's leaving him had he experienced much despair. What seemed to set it off this time was a run-in with a community leader, a very strong black woman who ended up calling Peter a racist.

He was sitting in their small room in despair over his lack of effectiveness in helping the community leader work through a crucial decision that affected the future of the community. But he was blaming her. A monologue was going on: She doesn't care. This situation is hopeless. What am I doing here, anyway? Where can I go if I leave? What a failure I am. What do you mean, "racist"?

He did not want to show weakness to Suzanne, so he asked a friend for help. All he said was, "Have you ever read Tillich's *The Courage To Be*?" Peter borrowed it from him and read most of it the same night. What he needed to hear came through: courage to accept one's acceptance is the same as the courage to accept one's despair. "The act of accepting meaninglessness is in itself a meaningful act. It is an act of faith."

He was being driven to despair, which was driving him to deeper faith, to the courage to be who he really was at that moment: a despairing, failing man at thirty-two. That was the first time he ever *really* heard that despair was good, even redemptive. Tears washed his being as he experienced the peace of "all is well." From somewhere he heard the all-important fact of life that he was accepted in the condition he was in – despair – and he said "yes" to that fact, breathed deeply, laid the book down, and fell asleep.

Did he go out and conquer the situation the next day? Not exactly, but he did have a new appreciation for the leader, a new perspective on the situation, and there for a while he was more effective in relating to most everybody around him. The black female leader told him he seemed different and easier to work with. She half-teasingly, half-seriously, told him he wasn't a bad racist, that "southern racists were better than yankee racists."

As Tillich pointed out, Peter was freed up to go back into the situation. He could have quit and left, but he "went out of himself, was empowered to transcend himself," under the impact of the Spirit in the midst of his despair. A life lesson he would remember.

And something else happened that he would

remember. He was at attention as the midwife said, "Peter, do exactly what I tell you when I tell you. The cord is wrapped around your baby son's neck."

He followed her every command and very adroitly helped her reposition the cord. Almost instantly the baby was born, in messy but beautiful shape. Peter fainted and crumpled against the wall. The midwife watched him go down but saw that it was an easy fall. When he woke up, Suzanne was cuddling their son, with an angelic smile on her face.

She said, "Dear, Peter, you helped save his life. Come here and meet our son." And then she added, "Are you all right?"

He didn't know he had fallen but guessed as much. He carefully reached for the bed and held onto it as he moved next to mother and child.

She said, "Peter, this is Adam, your Son. Adam, this is Peter, your Father."

He began to cry when Suzanne handed the little one to him. He was bursting with tides of emotion, both fear and joy. He had already been reminded how fragile Adam's life was. He reflected, what if I grow to love him so much and something happens to him? But won't it be absolutely wonderful to be with him and watch him grow up? He and Adam had to sit down, for the reflections were heavy.

Then Peter jerked his head up to look at Suzanne, whom he had completely ignored. He got back up, slowly moved to her and saw that she was also crying. He leaned over with Adam and the three of them had a love fest. Joy was ascending.

Peter said in her ear as he kissed her, "That was by far the greatest thing you've ever done and may ever do! Blessed is the fruit of your womb."

A few months later, as they participated in Daily Office – the staff's early morning service of worship in the old gym in the ghetto – Suzanne looked up at one of the huge wall hangings of saints, the one of Abraham, who was raising the knife in obedience to God, ready to offer his son as a sacrifice. She began to wipe the tears, for she knew her baby was not really hers.

But she was also crying because of the recently published staff assignments. She and Peter were assigned to Indonesia. They were told that Peter could go on ahead and Suzanne and the baby could join him later.

Now Suzanne was in despair. She had phoned her parents and told them, and they thought she was out of her mind. "How in the name of everything that is holy can you even consider such a thing? What do you mean 'assigned'? It's bad enough that your poor baby is in the ghetto as we speak, but why would you take a baby to somewhere like that? We don't even know where it is. Will you please come home? We'll buy you a ticket this very minute."

She tried spending her early morning worship time *not* looking at Abraham, but the very thought of God's command to him was never far from her mind. She shared all of this with Peter one night, as if he did not already know.

She said, "And what am I going to tell my parents?"

With compassion, Peter replied, "Tell them they should not have raised you up in the church. Tell them they should not have read you all those bible stories at bedtime. Tell them that God has not changed, that (Peter caught himself as he was about to say "he") God is the same God who called Abraham and Moses and Mother Teresa and all the others to be absolute in their obedience to (he caught himself again before he said "him") God. Tell them that we have heard the same call."

Suzanne said, "*You* tell them."

Peter put his arm around her, "What's this all about, anyway? You didn't even tell them you were here in the ghetto till weeks after you got here. Now all of a sudden you are bowing to your parents' wishes. What's going on?"

"Well, I guess I love Adam more than you do." And she began to sob.

Peter said nothing at that moment and just held her close.

The next evening as they went to bed, he opened up the subject with some trepidation.

"Suzanne, about what you said last night. You know I love Adam deeply. And you know that I am very attached to him, also. So what are you really trying to say?"

With heartfelt words she said, "I'm so sorry I said that, Peter. I don't know exactly what's happening to me, but I feel very torn inside. I guess my culture – our culture – and our understanding of trying to do God's will are at war. God and our culture are fighting over our bodies and spirits. It is so very hard. When I stop to think, I know what really makes sense, but when I get those phone calls from home, I forget what I've dedicated myself to be about. It would be so natural for us to go home, go to the bank and get a thirty-year mortgage, go back to the bank and get a loan for a car and all the kitchen appliances, take Adam to school and pick him up after school everyday until he goes to college, get back into teaching and do a fine career and hope Adam marries a fine girl and has us two grandchildren we can take out for ice cream regularly. All that doesn't make any sense to me anymore, but I still have this war down inside. Thank you for being so understanding. I love you very much. We have a great little family and we'll do what we know is right."

Then she added, "Why don't I wait until Adam is about six months before we join you?"

Peter gave her a big hug and kiss and said, "I think that's the right decision. Thank you for giving that powerful little speech. You know I love you very much. We'll be just fine . . . 'just mommy and me and baby makes three, we're happy in our blue heaven.' I wonder why the color is 'blue'? I hope it's not because the songwriter thought heaven was up there in the blue. But he wrote, 'we're happy *in* our blue heaven,' so he must have understood that heaven is right here, don't you think?"

Suzanne kissed her man and said, "You're a real blessing! Good night, Blessing. See you in my dreams. And I'm going to put something in my ears so I can't hear the wake-up gong. . . . But Adam will. Oh well, pell-mell, she slid down the hill and just missed hell."

Peter chuckled, "Where did that come from?"

"From my poetic self," she whispered. "Good night, out-of-sight, don't let the bedbugs bite."

***

From Ms. Mary's church they left by big black funeral hearse for the country graveyard where she would lie at rest. Peter was deeply brooding, remembering the first time he met her outside his church, the time he preached at her church and she named him "Journer." She was dressed in the same white outfit that she had worn then. He had stood by her open casket and touched her hand that she first stuck out to him asking for money, no, demanding money. He smiled inside as emotion rose.

At the graveside, well over a hundred gathered. A group of them started singing gospel hymns, and most all assembled sang along, even Suzanne as she held baby Adam. After they had finished the most moving and longest rendition of the "Sweet By and By" he'd ever heard, Peter stepped forward to remind them of the eternal truth on which they stood.

He began, "Mary came from God and returns to God. From everlasting to everlasting, she is God's. *Amen* ("Amen!" from all gathered). Death is part of life, or being in whatever form is being with God – from the beginning of eternity, to the now of eternity, to the end of eternity (Amen!).

"We believe the power of God was in the beginning, is now, and ever shall be (Amen!);

therefore, our form, whether dust or flesh or spirit, is breathed into being and sustained in being by God, forever (Amen!). We may wish to remain in the flesh forever, maybe fearing that we will go out of being (Yes!). Yet, even after the death of the flesh we are sustained in God's being (Amen!). We are always in God's being (Amen!). Praise be to God (Hallelujah!).

"Therefore, we prostrate ourselves before God and give praise as did Job.

> [At the news of the death of all his family, his attendants, and his animals] Job stood up, tore his cloak, shaved his head, and threw himself prostrate on the ground, saying:
>
> 'Naked I came from the womb,
> Naked I shall return whence I came.
> The Lord gives and the Lord takes [back];
> Blessed be the name of the Lord.'

"We believe in the resurrection (Amen!), by which we mean life triumphs over death eternally (Amen!), and therefore we believe that death is part of the good creation of God (Amen!). 'The Lord gives and the Lord takes [back]; Blessed be the name of the Lord' (Hallelujah! Amen!).

"We believe we can trust God above all else (Amen!). Hear these words of the

Psalmist." Peter recited the 23rd Psalm and many joined in.

"We also believe in the eternal love of God (Amen!)." He recited from Romans 8, "I am sure that nothing can separate us from God's love," followed by lyrics from "O Love that wilt not let me go."

"So, we are surrounded by these great words of witness to our God (Amen!), to the eternal truth that Mary and we are God's children (Yes, Jesus!), God's precious ones (Hallelujah!), God's loved ones (Glory!). This is the way life is. Praise be to God (Hallelujah! Amen! and clapping)."

He ended with a prayer: "Great Father of thine own (Yes, Lord!), into thy hands we commend our dear Mary (O sweet Jesus!), for none other is worthy of her safekeeping but thee (Amen!), to whom be all glory, laud and honor, through Jesus the Christ and thy Spirit. Amen and Amen (Thank you Jesus! Praise God! Hallelujah!)."

The choir finished with a lively "Hallelujah Chorus." Mary was still on the journey and Peter wished her Godspeed in his heart of hearts.

On their way back to Chicago, Suzanne held his hand and said, "My husband the preacher. I am so proud to be your wife you can even call me "Sister Suzanne."

Adam cried something that they took to be "Amen!" for he was probably sensing that he was a child of God on the great earth journey, and therefore named "Adam."

At his baptism the next week, they reminded all present that Adam was indeed God's child, always at home no matter where; that he was Jesus' little brother, born in original grace; and that his journey master, Spirit, is always present. Thus, he was baptized in the name of God the Father, God the Son, and God the Holy Spirit – surely a child of God.

Third World Baptism

On the anniversary of the assassination of Martin Luther King, Jr., Peter made his first flight out of the USA, from Chicago to Jakarta, via L.A., Anchorage, Tokyo, Hong Kong, and Singapore. From the time he left Chicago to the time he made his taxi ride to a hotel in downtown Jakarta, he knew he was out of his world.

He did not dislike foreigners, else he would not have been assigned to Indonesia, but he felt at least discomfort, if not anxiety. He was surely strange to them as they peered at him on the streets, in the shops, and especially in the villages where everyone gawked with little inhibition.

Peter and the staff already present were fortunate to be in Indonesia. The signature of the Foreign Minister was what made it possible. The staff training facility was set up at the adjacent village of relatives of the Foreign Minister, about forty-five minutes to a two-hour drive out of Jakarta, depending on the circumstances of weather and traffic.

During the monsoon season, the staff had to drive as far as possible in their dilapidated van, then take off their shoes, roll up their pants or tie up their skirts, and walk hand in hand through the rising muddy water to the project facility. Peter lost one of his rubber flip-flops pushing the van when it stuck in a foot of mud. He remembered passing so close to oncoming traffic that their rearview mirror was sheered off their van. And he well remembered the taxi van ride when the vomit from a child in front blew back in his face and all over his shirt.

He would never forget the trip when the taxi van hit a boy running across the highway, and the immediate retribution of the crowd as they grabbed the driver out of the van and held court – Peter slipped away to catch another taxi before the mob dispensed justice. He arrived at the Jakarta office late, cleaned up, put on his city suit to visit the chief executive of Indonesia's oil company, Pertamina, who wanted to know why Peter was living in a village like the one he grew up in, why a well educated and relatively rich American would give up his style of life and bring his family to such a situation. Why?

He asked with a curious smile, "Are you with the CIA? Or maybe you have a religious motivation?"

Peter felt he had to level with the cosmopolitan, English-speaking executive: "I personally have a religious motivation, as you say. As Indonesians believe in Pancasila and Muslims believe in care of others, especially the less fortunate, my belief sends me to serve by training the Indonesian staff to work for comprehensive village development to help the villagers raise their quality of life."

The executive was pleased with Peter's response and extended the fifteen-minute meeting to over an hour as they talked heart-to-heart about the future of the thousands of villages across the thousands of islands called Indonesia.

They both knew that effective human development was far deeper than what USAID and the World Bank delivered, for instance. The executive agreed with Peter that even though the expatriate staff could not promote their religious beliefs – else they would be kicked out – they could tap the human spirit of the people and release the motivation necessary to do authentic development.

He asked Peter how Pertamina could help.

Peter gave him his prepared request. "We need two things from you, sir: one, that Pertamina become a part of the village development venture by adopting a cluster of villages, with your local technicians volunteering their expertise when needed. Second, we need money to help pay the expenses of training Indonesian staff to lead village development efforts across Indonesia. If either of these requests is not within your giving guidelines, then I'm sure we can work out what is. Simply, we need expertise and money."

The oil man immediately gave his decision, "Yes to both requests. Write me a one-page proposal of your specific needs and we will help. You have my word. And one more thing: when you ex-pats need R&R, let my office know. We have many guest houses around the nation and especially in the Puncak mountain pass nearby. Thank you for coming, thank you for serving our villages, and I look forward to seeing you again soon.

"Oh, one more thing, you need to speak with my counterpart in charge of the Indonesian plantations. I will set you up. Oh, and you need to approach the international oil companies exploring here. I will set you up with Mobil right away. Let's tell my secretary to get onto all this before I forget what I've promised."

Peter was elated and felt they had made a big leap in securing the frame necessary to carry out their village development mission in Indonesia. They had the government authorization through the Foreign Minister's office. Now they were well on their way to having authorization from the quasi private sector. USAID was already making grants. They still needed more authorization from the regional and local governments and the religious sector.

Such support was necessary to help coordinate the village development among a network of village demonstrations – Human Development Projects, they called them – across Indonesian, first in Java, then Sumatra, then Sulawesi.

Peter's work was going extremely well, but he was exhausted when he met Suzanne and Adam at the airport. It had been a short six months for Peter and a long six months for Suzanne. To celebrate their reunion, they did go to the Puncak for three days before they were off to North Sumatra, preparing for a village project outside Medan by several hours, by bus and boat.

On the commercial outboard motor boat on their way to the village, they shielded Adam from the equatorial sun, but he enjoyed the spray of the water on his face and the attention of the local passengers, who could not keep their hands off him. Peter held him up, out over the side of the boat, when he had "to go," just as the locals did.

On board they were offered boiled pickled eggs and *kampung* chicken legs, with luke-warm tea served in glasses. Suzanne and Peter said "no" to the local delicacy of salted fish heads with eyes looking up at the one eating them.

The villagers and staff had spent weeks of preparation for the five-year planning consult to take place in five days in the village. The entrance to the village was lined with brightly colored banners on bamboo poles signaling that the planning consult was something really special. The villagers were honored that so many visitors were willing to come into their community to help them plan for the future.

Suzanne and Adam were a demonstration within themselves. Chubby-cheeked baby Adam was a big fascination for the village mothers, who through sign language asked what Suzanne fed the baby. This provided the visiting health workers opportunity to talk practically about the importance of nutrition for nursing mothers.

Besides the movement staff, the public, private, and volunteer sectors (such as local service groups and NGO's) sent representatives to live in the huts of villagers and go through an in-depth planning process of visioning, contradiction analysis, strategic proposals, and tactical actions for implementation. The key to all this was the input of the local sector, the villagers. Everyone else was there to help them build the plan and help them make it happen.

Most of the participants from outside had not stayed in a village at all, or not recently. They were deeply addressed by the poverty, and yet the sincerity, of the villagers, with their intuitive, practical savvy.

Peter and the international staff were orchestrating the event. Out in such a remote area, it was a Herculean task to put together a typed and duplicated first draft of a document for all participants, including charts and diagrams. Its presentation was awesome, especially to the villagers, most of whom could not read, but who knew their input of hopes and dreams for their village were recorded in "the book." They helped give the reports in the final plenary and present their newly written story and song and their new village symbol, which was in the front of the eighty-page document, and drawn large onstage.

The Governor of the Province gave a closing address to promise his full support. About twenty preschoolers, wearing sashes with their village symbol on them, sang a medley of songs just learned that week and ended with the new village song. The village preschool was now in being. The next generation was heralding the future. Their parents were bursting with pride. Most everyone else was secretively wiping their eyes, for this was a genuine revival relative to the future of the village, and the surrounding villages, since a major strategy was to make this a demonstration and training village for a cluster of villages.

Key to success after the consult was the bonding going on among the various groups of people from all the different backgrounds. To make sure implementation got off with a bang, cross-sector teams committed to do visible "miracles" the next weeks and to do ongoing development until the village made the turn to cohesive and effective development on its own. Third world development went amazingly fast when the sectors lined up, light-years faster than in a USA ghetto or rural project.

The Indonesian staff at the training center near Jakarta, a very proud lot, were struggling with the corporate life-style and being led by Americans, Australians, and a Chinese couple from Singapore. Thank goodness for two Indonesian English teachers who did most of the translation with the staff and in critical village meetings where a mistranslation could become a big issue, for example, "$500,000" instead of "$50,000" from USAID.

The Indonesian staff were young and full of idealism and emotions of all kinds, including romantic. It was not long before a

Christian young man from the island of Nias fell in love with a young Muslim woman from a nearby village. Peter and Suzanne did not encourage the relationship but did not realize what a cultural no-no it was. Everything moved fast. They were engaged on the no small condition that he would voice his commitment to convert to Islam during the wedding service.

With Peter, Suzanne, Adam, and other staff representatives seated in her family's living room, along with her relatives and close neighbors, the imam, her uncle, started the service. Things seemed to be going fine until the question was put to the young man to commit to Islam. He balked, she cried, the imam and father got angry. The staff saw the gravity of the situation and quickly exited with the groom, got in the van, and drove back to the staff facility without stopping – and mostly in silence.

Peter was advised by the headman of the village to take Suzanne and Adam to Jakarta, for the angry family was set on retribution. They had lost face and were blaming it on the leaders of the staff, especially Peter and Suzanne. The three of them were in Jakarta within a couple of hours, staying with friends they had met at the international school.

Within a few days they heard that the headman of the village, who was also the religious leader, had been able to pacify the angry family and secure their promise not to harm Peter's family or the staff in any way. The broken-hearted young woman went home to live with her family, never to be heard from again. The young man, it was agreed, must leave the island of Java and not return under any circumstances. He was assigned to work in the North Sumatra village training school and then a development project in Malaysia.

The whole incident understandably got to Peter. He sounded off to Suzanne, "What religious bigotry! All the '*My* religion is better than yours. You must convert to *my* religion or not live in *my* society. If you cross us, we will come after your family.' Religion divides rather than unites, and we cannot even deal with such fundamental questions here in the project. How will we ever be able to live together in one globe?

"But we know just as bad or worse. What about the religious babble of the KKK? Or how could white Christians in Alabama stand by and watch the blacks sprayed with fire hoses and the police dogs sicced on them, or how could they turn their heads when the black churches were bombed and the children killed? Or how could the mostly Christian Nazis kill 6 million Jews? Muslims, Jews, and Christians come from the same religious source in present-day Iraq. How did it all get so divisive?"

The Christian and Buddhist staff could not even mention their religion in the project and were advised by the local government to take down a symbol of the Iron Man from the village preschool wall, for it was thought to represent the Christian's resurrected Jesus. A bit of a Muslim zealot in the village had accused the staff of proselytizing the Muslim children. Nothing ever came of it except the admonition from the local government officials to be more careful.

As Peter was becoming less tolerant of intolerant Muslims, Suzanne asked him if he was a Judeo-Christian bigot? Was he going to be a part of the solution or live out Gandhi's quote, "An eye for an eye makes the whole world blind"?

Peter knew they had not dealt with the religious sector directly, and for good reason. Yet, how in the name of God, or Allah, were they ever going to reconcile such deep-seated religious bigotry?

He had plenty of time to brood on this question as he came down with an uncommon strain of malaria, contacted in the village consult in North Sumartra.

Pluriform Movement

In Malaysia, also part of the staff's geographical responsibility, one project, especially demonstrating economic development, was coming to an unusual end. The Minister of the State had asked the staff to come and help the village area where he was born; therefore, the government was fully behind the venture. But after two years, when the Minister was in the USA for a conference, the deputy Minister, who was a political foe of the Minister, gave the staff one week to leave. He told them that if they did not, he would send news to the global development community that they were a Marxist group infiltrating the villages.

This was a real blow to Peter and staff who realized that they were caught in the middle of an internal political ploy, yet Peter felt that the village was nearing self-sufficiency, so he recommended the local staff needed to bow out gracefully and immediately. In light of the immediate threats and the uncertainty of the Minister's response under the political circumstances, Peter's recommendation stood.

But that event did not begin to compare in

impact with the news that Joseph, founder of their ecumenical group and movement, had died. He was a man of vision for global renewal, beginning at the most local level, be it a ghetto or a third world village. Under his leadership, the movement in twenty years was in some thirty nations, with a staff of over two thousand, most economically self-sufficient in their assigned regions.

Joseph believed that all religions sing from the same songbook. His passion for creating a new religious mode equaled his passion for a new social vehicle, the *yin* and the *yang* of depth *human* development. In everything, he said, you are dealing with revitalizing the spirit of the people as you help them focus upon their own community's future as a demonstration to the communities of the globe. Together these presuppositions were the context for a global movement, binding together the hearts of people for the sake of bending history from the bottom up – a grassroots revolution built upon the ethos of care. He never let the staff forget that everyone cares, and tapping that profound care and making it demonstrable is what being a human is all about, is what human community is all about, from the family on out.

Joseph was near the top of Peter's list of saints, in spite of – or maybe because of – his demanding more of the staff than was humanly possible. He said life was for expending on behalf of all, and he spent his waking and dreaming moments strategizing ways for all involved in the movement to have a practical venture worth living and dying for. For example, he would say, what would it look like for the millions of buildings with steeples on them across the globe to relearn how to serve their communities, their parishes? What would it look like for millions of local communities to release the greatness of their people? What would it look like for every person to see a way to live his or her one great life? He said such were the real religious questions of the time.

Joseph's final rites were a celebration worthy of his zest for all of being. The mourning of the staff around the world soon turned to the struggle of filling the vacuum of leadership. The structures of corporate leadership of the movement were in place, but Joseph's charisma had been so great that the movement fell against the ropes after the blow of his unexpected death.

Since Peter and Suzanne had been effective leaders in Indonesia and Malaysia, they were assigned with an Indian couple to help lead the village movement in India. In one State alone they were working with a village project

101

in every county, or *taluka*, well over two hundred total, and several hundred young Indian staff.

Peter and Suzanne spent most of their time that first year on the road, traveling to the villages and revitalizing and reconnoitering the Indian staff. They had left Adam in the city at the staff headquarters while they were on the road. Though he was in an excellent preschool run by nuns, Peter and Suzanne felt guilty for being away from him much more than they had planned to be.

Suzanne and the female Indian leader that she shadowed spent much time catalyzing and nurturing the women, children, and youth of the villages. Peter and the male Indian leader he shadowed spent much time nurturing the leadership and strengthening the economic underpinnings of the village movement. Each traveled with a briefcase or shoulder sack filled with notebooks, a change of clothing, and toiletries. Peter had an inflatable pillow since they spent many a night sleeping on the ground floors of village huts or under the stars.

Suzanne and Peter eagerly looked forward to rendezvousing at a little hotel when they were on the road. They sat in the restaurant downstairs and shared a *lassi*, a refreshing yogurt drink, or ate *kulfi*, something like ice cream, as they gazed at each other across the table. They found such times together extremely passionate, but also full of sadness as they reflected on being away from their little boy, semi-adopted by a staff colleague and the nuns. Were they ruining his life, or was he getting a real education about life that most children in the West were missing out on? In any case, they longed to be with Adam.

What was getting clear to Peter was that as well as the eco-socio-cultural program benefit to the villages was the benefit of movement building in that part of the world. Staff and villagers of all ages were standing tall, including women and youth. They had a new vision and a way to engage. Transformed lives were happening in the corporate efforts across the villages through the pluriform movement: pluriform in economic and social status, in age and gender, in nationality, in religion, in worldview. They were demonstrating more radical pluriformity than the diversity in the USA. And it was all because of a life-and-death common mission.

But what was so perplexing to Peter, at the same time, was the struggle to articulate the depth dimension of life and to come up with the profound symbolic ways of rehearsing oneness. As they experimented with translating inspirational poetry, such as Tagore and Kazantzakis, into the local dialects, Peter dreamed of cloning the three or four Indian leaders who had the ability to translate with power the transforming images to the uneducated and educated, the nationals and foreigners, at the same time. Unless depth spiritual dialogue happened, the whole venture would go the way of all well-intentioned activist movements. People's spirits would eventually languish. He was thinking night and day about how to deepen the movement, how to help the staff and villagers see beyond short-term victories, beyond measurable success. How could he assist them in the development of their interior resources that would sustain them through the reality of the dark night and the long march that would surely come.

He recalled an experience told by Joseph that pointed to the wisdom he was seeking. On one of his visits to Indian before he died, he walked with two old men, one a Muslim and one a Hindu, as they looked for new water sources for their village. They discovered a deep bond, not through dialogue of language, but through looking into the deeps of each others' eyes as they went about their crucial task. Joseph said in the communion of several days together each fell down a different well – one Christian, one Muslim, and one Hindu – and were drenched in the common water table. Three wells, one river. He said that the three of them spontaneously embraced before he left, for they knew they were bound for all eternity. They knew they were one in Spirit.

Without that sort of movement of depth there would be no lasting movement, no transforming movement. Peter longed for the pluriform rituals, stories, songs, symbols that would bind this movement for the forty-year march through the wilderness. His constant brooding was on the future of this pluriform movement that must be built on Spirit most of all.

It was not long before the travel to the villages by train and bus, often third class, took their toll on Peter's health. His body weakened through acute dysentery that brought on a malaria relapse. He was in and out of local hospitals and guest houses furnished by the government, the religious, and the corporations that were helping support the village movement. His weight declined twenty pounds to 140. With his worsened health came a new bout of despair. He was finding it hard to function effectively. It was decided that Peter needed to go back to the USA for an extended time until he could recover his strength.

He was assigned to the annual meeting of the global movement in Chicago. As he hugged Suzanne and Adam goodbye, he knew they were strong and would do well without him. Yet, he felt he was abandoning them, even though he was to return within a few months.

Suzanne ceremoniously held his hands out in front of the two of them and said, "Peter, we send you out to be the great man you are and to tell the world about this great movement in India. *Namaste*."

Adam did the same as best he could, borrowing from his bedtime ritual, "Daddy, you be Iron Man in every situation (a word he could hardly say)." He finished with his hands together and a very deep and quick bow.

The three of them embraced as they stood among the throng at the Bombay airport. They wiped their tears, kissed, hugged, and waved goodbye until Peter turned through a door to board his plane.

Between naps on the plane, Peter was reflecting about his life and mission in India and what landed him there. More than the assassination of his President was the image of the Earthrise during the summer of '69, which he had witnessed on television during his first summer in the Chicago ghetto. An internal voice said, "All the money your country spent on getting that man on the moon was spent for you, Peter." Since then, he'd had his symbol and had stuck the Earthrise image in his briefcase to see every time he opened it.

There had been no boundaries seen from up there by the astronauts, just one Earth community to care for. But that significant symbol for Peter's journey took many years to become really grounded.

He was not the only one who knew that every person is called to global care. Peter recalled the night he and Udesh, a young village leader, had talked the night away. As they sat on the ground in the cool of the evening, outside his very humble dwelling – if they had gone inside they would have still sat on the ground – he told Peter about his studying mechanical engineering and going to Bombay to get a job. "I am one of the lucky ones," he said. He began to make money and was taking on the middle class life-style. One day a beggar came up to him, a man from a village like his, with his hand out. That seemingly small event was a turning point in Udesh's life, for he recalled his early vow to help lift his village out of poverty.

He went back to live in his village. He told Peter his vocation was living on behalf of the 500,000 villages of India. A few days later, in a speech to villagers and government officers from the area, who had come to visit his demonstration village, he said, "I am helping to develop my village on behalf of the 2,000,000 villages of the earth." Peter knew

Udesh's vocational symbol was the same as his, the Earthrise.

Looking out the window of the plane, Peter found himself rehearsing the words to a powerful movement song, to the tune of "Country Roads":

> At the center, aweful calm;
> Born of Spirit, then my life was gone.
> Human suffering over all the world –
> Five billion people die and never live.
>
> From the center we shall stand,
> In every nation, throughout every land;
> Building patterns to release the new –
> Dying daily that the new may live.
>
> *Refrain:*
> All the earth belongs to all:
> That's the vision and the call.
> Local people rise again
> To build the earth, the common earth.

His internal dialogue continued: Udesh was a Hindu and I was a Christian; he was a brown man and I was a white man; he was about thirty and I was a few years older – each deeply understanding the other as we talked about the vocational odyssey of our lives. We talked of how so many people never seem to get past the event that raises consciousness and wrestling. They never reach deep resolve. It's as if they get blocked and slide back into the shallows of life – and try to forget they've been called.

Peter fell asleep after they took off from Heathrow Airport and slept most of the way across the Atlantic. After he boarded the leg of the trip from Dulles International Airport, the smaller passenger plane flew low, down the sunlit Shenandoah Valley that spring. The view was another awesome moment of his life, so lush and green compared to the brown dust where he'd been in the villages of India.

Then a revelation. He realized the whole earth was his home. He had gone to the other side of the globe as a foreigner and was made to feel at home. He realized he did not love the USA any more or any less than he loved India and Indonesia. He was no longer a superpatriot, no matter how lush the USA seemed in every way at that moment. He had become a citizen of the globe.

Tagore's poetry was his poetry:

I came to your shore as a stranger,
I lived in your house as a guest,
I leave your door as a friend, my earth.

Poetry was spinning together . . . be it ever so humble, there's no place *called* home . . . every place on earth is home. He was experiencing universal gratitude and gratitude for his awesome journey thus far. He knew without doubt that he was being journeyed well.

Then Mary spoke, "We'll just call you 'Journer.'" He could hardly breathe he was so fulfilled. He closed his eyes and took several deep breaths before opening them again to the splendor of the valley and mountains outside his window. He wanted to shout "Hallelujah!" as they did at Ms. Mary's funeral.

Continuing
the Reformation

Peter did gain strength. Before long he was back up to 150 pounds. Instead of being assigned back to India, however, their family was assigned to their nation's capitol. What a shift. But why?

During several months of recuperating, he was gravitating back to his old calling, the Christian ministry. On one hand, that made no sense, being immersed in ecumenical, inter-faith, secular-religious living over the past number of years. But as he thought more about the spirit dimension of their global movement, and as he discerned the trends at their annual meeting in Chicago, he saw two things happening.

One, there was a strong push to share their methods with every group coming and going: communities, institutions, corporations, and governments. It was a natural outgrowth of the effectiveness of the methods, and more, it gave the staff a way to do the mission and earn their self-support at the same time. That certainly made sense, but not to Peter. He did not join the movement primarily to give society better planning methods.

Peter also observed a split in the priorities among the movement gathered. When Joseph was alive, he gave talks at the annual meeting – and every other place he went – calling the movement to never forget its primary purpose, to be a self-conscious part of the Spirit movement. He told them that their projects were to call people, no matter their station in life or their religion, to understand that the meaning of life was intentional spirituality and service. Now, without his leadership in their global movement, the "secular" was taking over.

He was caught. He felt he couldn't go back to a local congregation as a pastor. He resented membership drives and new building campaigns. That was out. But he felt he had to explore spirit methods more deeply and help contemporary seekers and non-seekers of whatever background to come to grips with the movement's foundational understanding that every situation was finally a spirit situation, calling forth intentionality and decisiveness on behalf of others.

In discussions, the Washington assignment made more and more sense to Peter. A protestant Bishop there that he had met was a strong friend of the movement and was asking for someone to be assigned to work with him in clergy training and local mission designs for multiple congregations.

Peter, Suzanne, and Adam were on their way to Washington. The Bishop arranged a shared office for Peter and Suzanne next to his, the use of a car, an apartment in the District that belonged to the denomination, and a modest salary. Monthly, Peter and Suzanne gave over half of it to the work of the global movement.

Adam, almost five, went daily to a black church kindergarten and fit right in. One day he asked his mom when his skin was going to turn dark. He had been in child care situations of color since he could remember. Suzanne reminded him of what he'd asked his grandmother the last visit when she made reference to a "colored woman." Adam remarked innocently, "Grandma, everyone is colored." So Suzanne reminded him that everyone was some color, and that he would probably stay the color he was, and that God loved all colors of people equally. She sang with him the song they had sung with preschoolder in the ghetto of Chicago, to the tune of "This Land Is Your Land," but as usual she felt she had to change the word from "man" to "ones":

We are the Black ones.
We are the Red ones.
We are the Brown ones.
We are the Yellow ones.
We are the Tan ones.
We are the White ones.

This is the land for you and me.

Chant:

Black ones! Red ones! Brown ones!
Yellow ones! Tan ones! White ones!
UNIVERSE ONES!

Adam liked the *Chant* – better, the *Shout* – the best as he raised his arms each time and did a cheerleader-like leap on "UNIVERSE ONES." Anyway, his question of color was answered for the time being. And the song was oft repeated as they went from church to church, a black church one Sunday or a yellow one or a tan one the next – but mostly a white one, even in a city that was predominantly black.

The launch event for the Greater Washington Cluster Experiment came in November when they guided all the clergy – and spouses, at Suzanne's suggestion – through a three-day planning retreat near Frederick, Maryland. As they pre-planned with the Bishop and the retreat committee, they hoped the clergy families would consense on working together in clusters of four congregations to enhance effectiveness, especially in local mission, which was hardly visible.

Needless to say, there was resistance. One clergyman said, "We have enough to do without taking on a whole new set of working relationships. Besides, my congregation won't buy in." From reflections in small groups several expressed the fear that there would be racial problems, especially since almost 25 percent of the churches were non-white congregations.

The Bishop was resolute, however. He and Peter and Suzanne created his presentation for the retreat. They came up with four strategies for the experiment under four "R's":

Rediscovery of the Word
Revival of spiritual discipline
Re-empowerment of the laity
Rededication to corporate mission

By the end of the Bishop's passionate presentation of the foundations of the experiment – which took about an hour – everyone was very clear that the Bishop was going to see the experiment through, whatever it took, for at least two years. Everyone present understood which way the wind was blowing and publicly bought in by the end of the retreat.

The twenty-four clusters of four congregations each had three strategic images:

training leadership cores in each congregation to meet weekly for planning and nurture; catalyzing eventfulness to build deeper congregational life together; and calling forth new mission within the greater parish of the four congregations.

It was Peter and Suzanne's responsibility to see that it all came off, knowing the devil was in the implementation. By the end of the first year, they had come up with a statement of ten contradictions that they had discerned among the congregations as they were in constant touch with them:

- *superficial understanding of the Gospel*
  (e.g., moral righteousness)
- *literalistic interpretation of the bible*
  (e.g., the creation story)
- *individual overemphasis*
  (e.g., personal redemption)
- *miniscule missional engagement*
  (e.g., dollars to missions beyond the local)
- *unfocused worship of God*
  (e.g., sometimes everything but worship)
- *paid ministers the only ministers*
  (e.g., unrealized ministry of the laity)
- *false messiahs*
  (e.g., looking for a better minister)
- *inauthentic covenantal discipline*
  (e.g., one-hour-a-week participation)
- *ineffective organizational structures*

(e.g., thirty-minute Sunday school)
• *humanistic operating patterns*
    (e.g., membership and building campaigns)

The list was every bit as applicable to the clergy families as to the laity, and finally a result of the culture of the contemporary church that was a cross between the supernaturalism of the middle ages and the shallow humanism of the modern secular age, with the real focus on individualism. And who was keeping the laity in bondage? The clergy, both wittingly and unwittingly. They were not clear, from the tradition and from their training in seminary, that the primary role of the clergy is to empower the laity in their ministry.

But Peter and Suzanne were drawing on every resource possible to keep from giving in to cynicism and impossibility. They were forever reminding each other and the Bishop and the clergy and laity that they were all figuring out how to again reform the church, not trying to tear it down. They repeated over and over, at every opportunity, that the key was thanking God for what is, as a part of the good creation, and daily rededication to reforming action.

When the "attack dogs" let loose on them – which was natural under the stress of reform – two things were definitely their defense. One, to attack the two of them was to attack the Bishop. Two, their dedicated life-style. Everyone knew that they were living on little to nothing and part of the Bishop's own salary. All three were walking the walk. The leadership of this experiment was committed.

What was coming out of this experiment besides the pain of change? At the first year's Greater Washington Cluster Experiment evaluation retreat, the group this time were the clergy couples plus two laity from each congregation, about 350 total. The group's list of reforms centered on a new image of the ministry of the laity, a new dedication to local mission, and a deeper commitment among clergy and lay leaders. The Bishop's closing remarks left them all with a summary quote to remember: "The church of Jesus Christ is made up only of ministers . . . of whom the clergy are a crucial part."

Reformation was underway. The second year was about training the laity for particular assignments beyond the traditional ones. Externally, they were assigned to research and analyze the needs of the parishes; to convene parish "town meetings" to vision, strategize, and celebrate the future; to catalyze parish care teams in conjunction with existing parish action groups; to help train parish leaders. Internally, they were trained and assigned to lead the new congregation team structure, which met at least quarterly; to help lead the newly formed monthly cluster Training School for Laity; and to set up weekly house church meetings. Though some churches, primarily because of ineffective and threatened clergy leadership, did not really participate, there was a new emphasis on the leadership of the laity in ministry that would forever change the culture of participating congregations.

The Bishop shared the results of the two-year experiment with other Bishops. It began to permeate the denomination and its seminaries. Peter and Suzanne passed on their documentation and step-by-step methods of the experiment to denomination leadership. Soon they were asked to set up and lead a national training lab in DC through the denominational seminary there. This way they could also continue to work with the Bishop's cluster churches, which would become training parishes for the seminary students and clergy and laity from across the nation.

What had started as a good idea among three persons was now affecting hundreds of churches and thousands of laity and clergy. The Bishop requested that six more couples from the movement be assigned to work with the experiment fulltime. Four couples were assigned. Along with Peter and Suzanne, they were dubbed the LCX (local church experiment) Team.

The Bishop, Peter, and Suzanne received more invitations to speak and train outside Washington than they could say "yes" to. The three of them had a strategic conversation before they really began to fly out to speak and to train in all directions. The Bishop wisely said, "We need to basically keep our theology to ourselves – it would only divide and divert attention from the task. No preaching or calling into question traditional ways. Just share our experiment of lay ministry and its methods. Keep it on the practical and the future. The crux of the new reformation will manifest itself in the change from a clergy-dominated structure to a lay-dominated one. Affirm the clergy in their role of calling forth and training the laity to lead. Remind all you meet that we are all good Protestants and are therefore still implementing the Reformation begun by Luther and company. We can't say 'priesthood of *all* believers' too many times. And remember, above all else, we are *not* prophets or saviors, just faithful reformers implementing tactics day after day, believing the kingdom of God is always at hand, present in our midst." Peter and Suzanne said "Amen!" in unison. Their ministry and that of the Bishopwas being transformed, as well as that of the lay and clergy they encountered. Democratization of the ministers of God was manifesting itself. They believed all were called and ordained by God, that all were *laity* – the people of God – that all could park in the "Minister" parking place: first-come-first-serve, as Peter used to say when he was a local pastor.

Transforming Event

Peter was leading more seminars at the seminary focused on the theory and practics of the Local Church Experiment and therefore spending less time directly with the DC experiment. He found the in and out refreshing. Suzanne and the other eight staff had the LCX in high gear as they worked together preparing a manual for publication and for seminary participants doing field work.

Because of Peter's effectiveness with methods and the response of the seminarians to his style of teaching, the seminary asked him to take a bigger teaching load. He was torn by being away from the church experiment but knew in his heart that he was definitely helping to prepare a new kind of clergy, one ready for the new reformation in the church.

He was entering a period of high creativity: writing articles for church magazines, doing interviews, preparing curricula, leading retreats, and speaking and leading seminars nationally and even beyond. He was up as early as 4 a.m. reflecting on the day ahead and beginning to write fuller entries in his journal. Writing was fascinating him, especially now that he was becoming adept at the computer word processor.

He began to let his imagination go and started playing around with book ideas, and one in particular, a Jesus book. He had promised himself back when he was in seminary he'd write a contemporary Christology. The idea took him over. He was spending his spare blocks of time doing authentic research for the first time in his life. It was not assigned. He was in the seminary library late and early, online browsing, and going through old notes of his mentor Joseph.

The Bishop, Suzanne, and Adam began to see the shift in his attention and said so. Peter simply replied that he had to do it and for them to be patient with him, that he was still heart and soul in the DC church experiment and being husband and father. Only thing is, he had taken on a fourth passion as well.

One early morning he listed the theologians whose Christologies had most influenced his own. Once he had listed twenty and reduced that number to ten, he had a real rationale for his research. The librarians at the seminary spent time borrowing books from all over since they did not have nearly enough resource books for his project. He skimmed and read well over two hundred books within six months as he took notes for those ten chapters of the book that got to the heart of each theologian's message that had made a lasting impression on his thinking and belief.

His Christology was becoming clear (which he started typing with a small "c" for several reasons, mainly because most writers did not capitalize the word "theology"). For a test run, he included the following in his sermon at a seminary chapel service.

I personally believe that Jesus the Christ is the most important happening in human life. But what does that mean? There are as many Christ images or christologies as there are humans interpreting the meaning of Jesus the Christ for their lives. Part of that meaning comes from the history of Jesus and the early church's memory of him as recorded in the New Testament on through the early councils. But the most important part of the meaning comes from our personal answer to the question Jesus asked, "Who do you say that I am?"

Willi Marxsen says that "christology" began when Jesus Christ catalyzed faith in the first believer. I agree with Marxsen that christology is all about faith. The crux of christology is this: we are brought to faith in "God" – or whatever word you choose to call that final reality or mysterious power at the heart of all that is. That's why I italicize the word "God," to remind us that we are naming that reality just as Jesus did when he called it "Father" or feminists do today when they call it "Mother."

Saying it as simply as I know how, christology is about our faith in that ultimate power, whatever you call it. Christology is about the events of our journey that call our faith into being and keep renewing it.

Lest you think I'm just talking about Christians, christology is a universal and timeless event. Paul, Augustine, Luther, Wesley, and I benefited from the same event as Abraham, whose descendents are Muslims, Jews, and Christians: or Muhammad experienced the same event as Moses and Jesus. The event of faith is the same reality for all who have ever lived, because the essential dynamics of existence have not and will not change. One comes to faith in "God," "Allah," "JHWH" the same way. The event is forever the same, coming from the heart of creation.

Does one have to believe a certain way? No. Does one have to join a certain religion or denomination? No. Does one have to do anything to be saved? No, only have faith in "God" (Peter gestured quotation marks). But remember, faith is sparked by an event from beyond our power that we say "yes" to.

Was Jesus brought to such faith? Yes. Does the event happen to a Buddhist, Taoist, or Confucian? Yes. Does the event happen to an atheist? Yes. Does it happen to a child? Yes. Any human is encountered by the dynamic we're talking about and through it can be brought to faith in "God," if he or she but chooses for life as it is, which is always full of grace.

Putting it all together, the christological event is personal, historical, universal, timeless, secular, religious, ecumenical, ultimate, and fulfills our deepest longings.

Christology is not about my having to believe that Jesus did certain things for me; not about my having to do certain things for Jesus. That is Jesusolatry. To follow Jesus authentically, I follow him in his faith in "God." That's the point of Jesus for me, that he epitomized radical faith in "God" and shows each of us that faith is always already possible, even on a cross. "Jesus Christ is Lord and Savior," or "Jesus is the Christ," means that I can trust "God" just as Jesus did. I don't have to believe anything special about where Jesus came from, where he went after he died, or whether he's coming back – those things may be interesting to speculate about but hardly crucial for our faith in "God." The Jesus Christ event brings us to faith in "God."

As I reflect on what makes most sense to my faith journey within the Jesus Christ tradition, I experience the *christological event* of life in three ways: I call them the grace event, the truth event, and the transparent event.

The *grace event* is about the human situation of separation, the happening of grace, and faith as acceptance. "Simply accept the fact that you're accepted" is how St. Paul and Paul Tillich say it.

The *truth event* is about having my illusion broken. "To die is to live" is how my mentor Joseph said it.

The *transparent event* is about our human blindness and sometimes being given to see. Everything and every event is a window – a transparency – to the power at the heart of creation, or "Seeing is believing."

These are three ways of illustrating life's big event that happens time after time – therefore "events" with an "-s." This event of Jesus the Christ – at the heart of Christianity, humanness, and creation – is not a belief system, is not magic, is not the property of any religion or Christian subgroup. The event of Jesus the Christ is the primal event that all humans experience: it is at the center of our lives and always will be. This event brings us to faith, wholeness, and reunion as we say "yes" to it.

The sermon caused a stir that was immediately manifest by several students walking out and also by many boisterous "Amen's." Polarity was evident. Dialogue groups were scheduled later in the week as the buzz intensified. Some students almost came to "un-Christian" blows during the articulation of their competing christologies.

Peter passionately hoped his book would help readers, especially seekers, re-image Jesus Christ. His idea for the book's subtitle he borrowed from Kierkegaard, that all humans are "contemporaneous" with the same power at the heart of existence that Jesus knew, that fills every human's journey with life-changing eventfulness and calls forth faithful obedience to God. The title he was less sure about at the moment. He was equally unsure of its publisher, until one fateful day in a conversation with a professor friend about the book.

He asked Peter, "Any luck with a publisher, and if not, would you like a good lead?"

"You've got to be kidding."

"I know a guy pretty well, and I'll give him a call and let you know if they are interested."

"Thanks a million."

Within the week, the friend stopped Peter in the cafeteria and gave him a number to call.

"They just might be interested."

Peter glided back to the apartment and told Suzanne, who jumped into his arms before she backed away and said, "Now, don't get your hopes too high. I understand it takes light-years to land a publisher, especially the first time."

She grabbed him by the hand, "Let's pick up Adam and go to the ice cream parlor and celebrate."

A few days later, the publisher rep called and made an appointment for lunch. He would be in DC for another appointment.

The day came. The conversation was easy. He asked Peter to send a rough copy of what he had so far and a brief description of the rest. They talked no time-line or money. Peter had no clue as to what to ask anyway.

About ten days after he had sent the packet of his book material, he received a phone call from the rep with a "yes," depending upon a pre-contract that both parties agreed on. And, yes, there would be a reasonable up-front signing check.

Within four months, with the help of the publishing company, Peter had submitted a polished draft that would number about 300 published pages total. Over the next couple of months of back-and-forth, he had a proof in hand.

Within another three more months, they had published the first run and wanted him to make a small promotion tour with some media interviews.

Peter was a proud new author. To celebrate and inaugurate the fact, Suzanne and Adam got to go with him to New York for a few days to begin the promotion of his new book, *Transforming Event: Contemporaneous with Jesus*.

During their time in New York, religious reporters grilled him, some not so traditional and some quite traditional. In the first group he got a very favorable interview. In the second, he and the book were roasted. He couldn't believe the slant they put on it, as though he were an unbeliever, even an atheist, talking about "the mysterious power that Jesus called 'Father.'" They wrote,

> Why does the author avoid the word "God," or when he uses it, he puts it in quotes? Does he believe in God or not, or does he believe in some new-age power? Why the word games? He says Jesus did not know nor use the word "God." He says he is trying to appeal to the "un-churched Christians." Is there such a thing? The bigger question, Is *he* really Christian?

Suzanne wanted to hunt the writer down and have it out. She growled, "What a righteous, Christian prig!"

When they got back to DC, the Bishop was more insightful: "You know, Peter, this will get you a lot of press. Maybe even get more reporters interested in the Local Church Experiment. Maybe even get us more of an international audience."

Peter was interviewed on air by a conservative Christian radio talk show host.

"So, why is your description of Jesus so alien to conventional Christian wisdom? I read your book and think you have wrapped up your existential philosophy in Jesus Christ clothing."

Peter, "You probably agree with me when I say with St. Paul that we Christians think grace is the center of our faith."

Host, "That depends on your definition of grace."

Peter, "Fair enough. Grace is what happens to us when we are deeply feeling our separation from God, neighbor, and self. Then, sometimes, it's like a voice says to us, 'You are accepted just as you are, sinfully estranged. You don't have to do anything but accept the fact that you're accepted, loved, forgiven – right now.' That is being struck by grace, and you and I have experienced it time after time, in big ways and small."

Host, "That certainly is a mouthful. Why can't you just use the old-fashioned words?

Why can't you just say "I accept Jesus as my Lord and Savior?"

Peter, "I have been describing grace as Paul, the first writer of the New Testament, did in his letters, especially the one to the Romans. Paul preached, wrote, and died before the first of the four Gospels, Mark, was ever written. That's pretty old-fashioned, wouldn't you say? And he said we are saved by grace, through faith, for works of love. That's the very beginning of the written Christian tradition."

Host, "Wrong. Every Christian knows Matthew was the first book of the New Testament. After our conversation here I am convinced you are playing games and are not what I call a born-again Christian. You sound like an academic, liberal 'Christian.' I'm very leery of your type.

"But, anyway, we are out of time. I won't say 'come back,' but will say we do earnestly hope you do have a saving experience of Jesus Christ. Until then, I'm *not* recommending your book to our listeners. Best they save their money for the offering plate next Sunday."

After they signed off, the host stuck his hand out to Peter and said, "I hope you will forgive me for being honest. That's the way I am. And, I might add, it does get me an exceptional Christian audience."

Peter shook his hand and thanked him for the interview. When he got home, Suzanne was angry: "I'd like to get my hands on that pseudo-Christian so-and-so!" Peter smiled and wanted to ask her what she'd do to him, but let it pass.

Adam had listened to the radio interview, also. As a rising high school student, he had much more developed reflective abilities than most because of being around his parents, who were always asking him questions rather than telling him the answers.

He asked his dad to have a heart-to-heart talk that weekend. Suzanne was on a Local Church Experiment seminar in Ohio. Dad and son decided to hang out together all day Saturday. After breakfast, they sat together in Adam's room, after Peter helped him tidy it up.

Peter, "So, how do we begin this chat?"

Adam, a little uncomfortably, moved to his bed and lay back, tossing a tennis ball in the air. "I've been thinking about my vocation lately and guess I want to know how to go about choosing one, or it, or whatever."

Peter, "What does the word 'vocation' mean to you?"

Adam, "I've heard you and Mom talk about it. I guess it means what your life's all about."

Peter, "Good. And how do we get to that point? Do you remember hearing any stories

I've told of how I was called?"

Adam, "The one about the President's assassination."

Peter, "That was one for sure. What were the steps of that vocational calling for me, if you remember."

Adam, "You were overwhelmed and felt you had to go to seminary to prepare to make a difference in society."

Peter, "Right. Anything else?"

Adam, "It was painful for you and it took a lot of courage for you to do what you knew you were called to do."

Peter, "Anything else."

Adam thought a minute or so, "And Mom left you because it wasn't her calling at that time – and later she caught up with your calling with one of her own."

Peter, noticing that Adam was really into the conversation, said, "And then what happened?"

"Ya'll reunited and gave birth to me."

Peter beamed and walked over and mussed up Adam's hair and said, "The day you were born was one of the happiest days of our lives."

Peter began to walk around the room. "Would you say you have been called?"

Adam, "Nothing as dramatic as yours, but sort of, I guess."

Peter, "Can you think of anything that has

happened to make you start thinking about your vocation lately?"

Adam, "Reading your book."

Peter was not expecting that. "How so?"

Adam, "Well, the way you talk about life-changing events that happen to everyone, little ones and big ones. I guess I've had a little one in just reading your book, the way it has made me remember times when I really felt accepted and forgiven. I'm pretty sure I've experienced grace. And you know what? It makes me think about how I can be like you, telling and writing about grace, which is about the most important thing a person can do."

And Adam stood up and hugged his dad. Neither would ever forget this little-big event.

Along Came Thomas

Peter wrote and taught more and more and did the Local Church Experiment less and less. Adam was a freshman on scholarship at a Presbyterian college to the south a good day's drive, where he was taking a course in environmental studies. That Christmas he gave his dad a little book – with Adam's high-lighting in it as a bonus – they'd studied by Thomas, a leading prophet of the earth community, to which everything belongs and is elected, not just humans – in other words, one of God's chosen planets. Adam and Peter later read together a book by one of Thomas' famous students, wherein the two main characters, Thomas and Youth, are in dialogue about the wonder and meaning of the universe.

Peter read in Thomas' books that human history is but a small part of earth history, which is a small part of universe history. We emerge from the universe and humanity – not just family, race, and nation. Peter was reminded of Max Ehrmann's lines, "You are a child of the universe no less than the trees and the stars; you have the right to be here." A different perspective, for sure: humans have the right to be here, *also*, because they are no less than the trees and the stars. Humans are no less sacred than trees and stars as far as universal equality is concerned.

These ideas started to ruminate in Peter and after a while began to reshape any vestige of Augustinian hierarchy: God above the angels, who are above the humans – the *only* ones made in God's image – and finally everything else, all created to be *used* by humans.

Thomas was about redefining the human. He wrote of the human venture within the earth venture. He wrote that humans have a very special role. Only humans, as far as we know, reflect upon and appreciate the totality of creation. And a big part of the uniquely human role is to vision and help implement the care systems for the earth community and its atmosphere. We in the West, especially, must be re-brainwashed to this big reality if we want the earth as it is to last for our progeny.

Out of his understanding, Thomas was writing that humans are only effective if they enter the sacrificial mode, not just to save themselves but the whole earth community.

Thomas' *universe understanding* would revolutionize *governance*. Humans would move from democracy to biocracy, shifting from human rights to creation rights. All life forms would be represented in parliaments, congresses, and constitutions, if all "subjects" – Thomas' word for what most call "objects" – were to survive.

. . . would revolutionize *economics*. Human technologies would be replenishing earth technologies rather than destroying them, for if nature goes into deficit – guess what – so do humans. What will it cost to purify the waters and the atmosphere? More money than humans can put together. Peter reflected that "pay later" is a sinful economy in the context of sustaining the earth community. No god is going to save it if humans destroy it.

. . . would revolutionize *education*. Recontext it all, not for job preparation and human fulfillment, but for quality of life in mutuality with the earth community. There would not be a measly course or two on ecology, but all courses would be learned in the context of the well-being of the total earth community.

. . . and Thomas' universe understanding would revolutionize *religion*. He asks why major religions are not demonstrating effective responsibility for the fate of the earth. If religions are to survive, they must bring about a reinterpretation of all their teachings within the context of the universe. Yet, most religions, especially Christianity, are still overly concerned with personal salvation, not planetary salvation.

139

It occurred to Peter that Thomas is talking about loving the neighbor with a capital "N." "Who is my neighbor?" is still the right question but is different 2000 years later than the parable of the Good Samaritan that Jesus recounted. Who is the Neighbor? Answer: the universe, earth, humanity, mine, and me. What does it mean to love the Neighbor? To sacrificially live on their behalf. Jesus did not say love humanity only. John 3:16 knew better than that. Jesus said one cannot love God and hate, kill, or destroy the Neighbor. Thomas was bringing forth a new dialogue about the first and second commandments as he talked about the mutuality of all things in creation as the primary law. Thomas was redefining theology and morality.

Peter propagated this new understanding at every chance. In Chicago he preached,

> Scripture is not saying love humans as yourself, but creation as yourself. Most churches, mosques, and synagogues are focused on deities; and consequently their members have little focus on care of creation. I haven't seen a single piece of Earth décor, an Earthrise image, for example, in any sanctuaries I've been in lately. Is worship just about my God and me?

Revisiting John Donne's poetry, if earth's species go down the drain by the tens of thousands each year, then so do I. God does not care mostly for me and mine? That is not biblical. According to my bible, God cares for all of creation.

Let us remember our origin, aim, and destiny. We are a piece of creation, which is the essential context of our vocation during our life journeys. Spirituality is found in the relationships of creation.

And one final thing: creation is not grim but full of goodness and life-giving energy, for Spirit is at the heart of creation.

Thomas was saying everything is *not* referent to the human, yet he was saying that the human's experience of Spirit's numinous presence in creation would rebalance the relationship between humans and the larger community. Thomas saw a new trinity of Spirit, nature, and humanity. He was saying that creation is the place where ultimate communion takes place, where divinity makes itself known. Universal creation is still *very good* in every sense of the word, as says Genesis – and Thomas, in his version of the creation story.

Through Thomas it was being revealed to Peter that he was a human bigot, whereas before he had come to know himself as a Christian bigot. He had a lifetime of repenting to do and he was trying to catch up.

Peter's next book on the universal spirit journey was another step in repentance, a way to remind himself and others that human domination of creation was an abomination. The book did not pick up where the christology book left off, but was a context for and extension of it. Peter understood better than before that the transforming power of the Christ event was from everlasting to everlasting for all that is – what St. John meant in the prologue to his Gospel by the Christ "came into his own creation." The grace event – or Christ event or God event or Spirit event – had come to be in the beginning and would last forever universally, forever "eventing" creation. Peter chuckled and called himself an "eventist," for he knew in his heart that the transforming event was the most important thing in creation. And he knew that this numinous event called "God" or "Christ" or "Spirit" always meets us in the midst of all that is, but is not any of it – the true mystery of "in but not of." So his christology of his first book was shifting in metaphor to "Spirit" – Peter never once hesitated in interchanging the three dynamics of the trinity.

He started using the word "Spirit" because

he wanted to make sure anybody and everybody who read his books knew he was not a traditional Christian. "Spirit" was the most universal religious word and therefore the least divisive. He sometimes capitalized it and sometimes used lower case and italics, which he preferred because he sensed it communicated better that *spirit* is not other-worldly but this-worldly, in the sense it's always present and happening here and now. Peter was obsessed with the truth that *spirit* is the primal energy of creation. He knew full well that Christianity and other religions had relegated *spirit* to the boundaries of creation rather than the center.

Therefore his vocation: to speak for *spirit* at the heart of creation that is eternally transforming creation. And by so speaking, he was fulfilling his earlier vocational poetry, being "evangelist" and "reformer." "Trans-former" seemed even better poetry now.

This second book was hard to pigeonhole as a category: religion, spirituality, inspiration, even ecology, because it was a lot of each. He and his editor ended up with the category "spirituality" on the back cover.

More book promotion trips followed, and again some were arranged as family outings as well. Adam was really into this book and the tour because he had a major responsibility for Thomas' influence on his Dad's thought. Adam listened intently to Peter's presentations of the book and the question and answer periods afterwards.

During the Atlanta trip, Adam stood up and moved to a mike – Suzanne about fainted – and made his own little speech when he thought his Dad had been abused by a questioner who called Peter an "atheist."

At the mike in the big Barnes and Noble bookstore, addressing some two-hundred crammed into a large room, Adam said, "Hello. my name is Adam and Peter is my Father. I'd like to speak to the last person who said my Dad is an atheist. I'm not sure what the young lady meant by that word, but he's definitely not an atheist. I live with him and I know. A better word for him – and me and my Mom, too – would be 'heretic,' (there was a roar of laughter) which literally means – as I found out recently in my college library – one who picks and chooses the parts of the tradition that make sense. That's the way it is with my Dad. He's thought a lot about what he's experienced, not just about what he has thought – if you understand what I mean. And he doesn't want you to swallow what he writes whole. He told me one time that I could only believe what I honestly believed, not what I was supposed to believe. My Dad is no fake. He believes what he believes because he's been there. He knows Spirit. He's no atheist. Thank you, and I'm sorry, Dad, if I've said too much. Back to you," with a nervous wave of his hand.

Peter could not say anything because of the applause, but also because of the impact of Adam's remarks. He got hold of himself and followed up, "Thank you, Son. Maybe I should let you start standing in for me up here." More applause.

The young woman who made the "atheist" comment got up and started to leave, but Peter said, "I hope you will not leave. Dialogue is the answer to our differences, not giving in or leaving. I hope you will stay and even go back to the mike and continue where you left off."

She hesitated and started to say something but left the room quickly, with head down. There was a hush in the room.

Another woman came to the mike. "I just wanted to say I wish my college daughter could hear the dialogue going on here. She has left the church and was pushed out, I believe, by those who say you have to believe this or that, period. So I really heard what your son was saying and wanted to ask him to come home with me and help me talk with my daughter."

There was laughter. The crowd seemed to be responding to the authenticity of Peter and Adam's witnesses. More than half of the audience lined up to get Peter to sign his book. Peter asked Suzanne and Adam to chat with them in line before they got to him. That slowed the line but made the event highly personal. Peter and company were on their way to a good seller, if not a bestseller, especially when they heard that the presentation and comments had been video taped and would be used in television and bookstore promotions.

Two weeks later he was being informally interviewed on a famous afternoon TV show, along with Adam and Suzanne. But such publicity brings out the wolves. Conservative and fundamentalist talk shows were on the attack calling him worst things than "atheist." One preached on Peter's "anti-Christ book." Another called it "non-Christian, new-age palaver that has to be stopped, in the name of God." Peter got rough phone calls from "Christians" and had to change the phone number. He was causing a stir, especially in the Bible Belt.

The Bishop talked with him and Suzanne at some length about all the negative com- munications from his churches, especially pastors who were getting it from their parishioners. Some were threatening to drop out of the Local Church Experiment.

Bishop, "Peter, you could become a sensation for Jesus in our day. That's both good and bad. I have received some positive communications from people locally and nationally. Some want to sign you up as a speaker. My question to you is, What do you see as your immediate future with the Local Church Experiment? I know you have been consulting with me and the other staff and have been leading LCX seminars at the seminary, and still going on a few LCX speaking engagements. But maybe it's time for you to bow out formally and just act as my consultant, leaving Suzanne and the other staff to run it – which they're already doing. I know it's not the center of your focus these days. You talk it over and let's see where we go from here. By the way, I hope you know I'm very proud to know you and sense what's going on in your writing and speaking – and teaching – is led of the Spirit. You are being used, powerfully."

Peter and Suzanne were quiet on the way home and as they prepared for bed, but the conversation began in earnest that night. They decided Peter would in fact teach, speak, and write, and she would become the designated leader of the LCX if that suited the Bishop and staff. They would suggest a six-month checkup and reevaluate where they were at the end of twelve months.

During that year, Peter and Suzanne and Adam spent part of a week with Thomas at his center on the Hudson and began a collegial relation that would grow over the years. Peter began a new book. Suzanne spent much time on the road setting up and monitoring Local Church Experiments in the USA and Canada. And Adam began a major in world religions and wrote an impressive term paper on "Ecological Disinterest Among World Religions."

At the end of twelve months the merry-go-round started. The Bishop was reassigned to another area. Adam had been accepted to do a masters degree at an Ivy League university in inter-religious studies, with a focus on ecology. The National Council of Churches had convinced Suzanne to work with them to further set up and monitor the Local Church Experiment – despite the fact she had no seminary or doctoral degree – along with two of the present eight staff. And Peter had arranged with Thomas to spend more time at his center as a place to write and a time to be in ongoing dialogue with him. Peter and Suzanne lived near New York City, not too far from Adam.

The years in DC were a major turning point in Peter's spirit journey. He was being the church with an impact. He was delighting in the vocational journey of Adam, who had helped give his father the biggest context yet through an introduction to Thomas' thought. And Suzanne had been yoked with Peter in vocation as they could not have imagined years before.

Peter was just past his fiftieth birthday and was living the profound journey along with his family as they participated together in common mission.

Creation-centered Development

As he talked with his colleague in the global movement, Peter realized that he had journeyed beyond where they used to be.

Colleague, "What the hell you mean that 'human development is a reduced context for the global mission'? That's all you've been doing in the ghetto and in those village projects in Indonesia and India. And that's all you've been doing in DC with the church reformation project, or whatever you call it. What else is there but human development? You sure as hell aren't developing animals or oceans or galaxies."

Peter didn't want to be in this conversation and wished he'd not said "reduced context." He replied, "By 'human-centered development' I simply mean humans are not the ultimate reason for development, and that a well developed human being cares for the whole earth, which includes the almost 6 billion humans, of course."

Colleague, "You sound more and more like a pantheist."

151

Peter, "No, I might be a 'pan-en-theist,' 'all-in-God,'as Hartshorne defined the word. And by that he meant God is not identical with the universe. But I prefer to say *spirit* is at the heart of all that is, trying to unite it all."

Colleague, "And you're sounding more and more like the guy we studied, you know, the one who wrote *The Phenomenon of Man*. A little far out for me. Anyway, we're not on the same wavelength.

Peter hesitated, "*The Human Phenomenon* is the better title for his book, which is about the human's role in creation, or what Thomas talks about with the human venture within the earth venture. That's the big context for human development."

Not really listening, the colleague said, "Whatever. By the way, can I tell them back in Chicago that you and Suzanne are still to be considered for global assignment?"

Peter, "We see ourselves as 'extended members,' that category that continues to evade consensus. We will continue to support the movement with our 'prayers, time, and resources,' as we used to say in our church vows."

Colleague, "So you're *not* up for global assignment?"

Later, when Peter went through the conversation with Suzanne, she was reflective as she said, "I wish extended membership was in place. I guess we'll just have to help bring it into being. Think of the hundreds of folks just like us who want to engage with a committed core of spirit people in a great global mission."

Over the next eighteen months, Peter was hard at work finishing the third book, with the co-authorship of Suzanne this time. They spent a long weekend with Thomas at his center talking about "communion" and "inter-communion." Peter was spending his time writing about the dynamics of the two big words. Suzanne, along with her other work, was pulling together reflections about life, many of which Peter had written when he was preparing a book not yet published. She was also writing other reflections from her journal.

Peter was expressing the relationship between the life-changing event of his first book and the universal spirit journey of his second. He wrote that communion experienced by humans and their intercommunion with all beings are the two core dynamics of authentic spirituality. Instead of a metaphysics of God up there or out there, he was articulating the spirituality of relationship in creation, guided by the *I-Thou* understanding, saying that relationship of whatever kind – with loved ones, even with the enemy, a dying species, or the 'Eternal Thou' – is where *spirit* happens.

Mixing and stirring it all together, he had come up with a new daily ritual that he and Suzanne – and Adam, when he was home – did together.

I.   I bow to all as *thou* this day,
       Namaste . . .

       in the name of *spirit*
       at the heart of creation,

II.   at the heart of all that is:
              all universes,
              our universe,
              mother earth;

III.   at the heart of all beings:
              all species,
              all humans,
              and my own being.

IV.   I bow to all as *thou* this day,
       Namaste (repeat four times).

***

Body motions made it more meaningful:

I. standing upright, slight bow, with hands
    together at the heart (Indian style)
II. arms upstretched, turn in all directions

III. upper body bent over, arms hanging
down, gradually touching the ground
IV. standing upright, slight bow, with
hands together at the heart

This rehearsal was guiding his relationships more and more, offering him the decision to relate to any and all others at any time as *thou* rather than *it*, expressed through the images of communion and intercommunion. Peter wrote:

Intercommunion . . .

. . . is the way life essentially is

. . . is the fundamental fact of the oneness
of creation

. . . is born out of an experience of
communion

. . . is a covenanted "yes" to creation

. . . is an *I-thou*, not an *I-it*, relationship
with what is

. . . is a demonstration of unity

Intercommunion is of the *spirit*. Most of what we humans know and do today is not in touch with *spirit*, is not uniting the billions of us, much less the universe of us. Let us be agents of intercommunion.

The publisher of the first two books was letting the two of them go at their own pace, sending checks regularly, which they lived on and shared with the movement and Adam, who was taking a term abroad in India as he researched Hinduism and Buddhism firsthand. He sent them a quote from Einstein that added insight to their book brooding:

> Buddhism has the characteristics of what would be expected in a cosmic religion for the future: it transcends a personal God, avoids dogmas and theology; it covers both the natural and spiritual, and it is based on a religious sense aspiring from the experience of all things, natural and spiritual, as a meaningful unity.

They were especially struck by the phrases "cosmic religion," "avoids dogmas and theology," "natural and spiritual as a meaningful unity."

Peter was finding a new articulation,

> There is, behind the multiplicity of events and evolving forms of creation, simply one power – and it appears in and through all, making of creation a hologram,

reflecting its likeness. All are transparent to *spirit* as ground and background; therefore, we can experience *spirit* in and through all phenomena and events of universal existence, sometimes dramatically changing our lives as humans.

Peter was transcending traditional religions, dogmas, and theology, not abandoning them. But he was passionate about transforming the religious orthodoxies that divide and demean creation, dividing it into righteous and sinful, good and bad, *thou* and *it*. He was declaring universal grace in a contemporary way. All is good, all are acceptable, the past is approved, and the future is open, as Peter and his laity rehearsed in the parish leadership colloquy way back when – a cosmic statement that he did not fully realize at the time.

As far as ethics is concerned, he was realizing that what is not in tune with *spirit* divides – most especially flippant religious talk that says we're the chosen and you're not, we have the way and you don't, we know "God" and you don't. Peter was offended by "God bless America" poetry that does not include the rest of creation; by the statement "except for the grace of God there go I," as if grace is given to some and not all; by "no one comes to the Father but by me" – unless one understands Jesus to have been saying that "only by loving God and all the neighbors of creation are you acting at one with the kingdom."

The truth be known, Peter was moving to a post-religious phase of his spirit journey. Instead of "believe this and do that in order to be saved," he was rehearsing "You are always already saved." He admired the phrase "original blessing," a play on "original sin," which was fallacious baggage to Peter. All of us are originally and eternally blest. Are we usually attuned to *spirit*? was the big question and what drove him to yearn to help get a new kind of spirituality into mass consciousness.

Creation is graced, yet there was a big problem with the meaning of words. Creation was a good word that had been hijacked by the religious right in the USA, called "creationism." They were determined to move away from "evolution," as personified for them by Darwin and Einstein, back to the 6-thousand-year history of creation in the Old Testament – significantly different from the nearly 14-billion-year history of the universe pointed out by scientists and Thomas.

"Creation" was for Peter not a meta-physical word but an evolutionary word, talking about the creative process going on from the beginning till whenever in the future, the process that stars and amoeba and humans were all participating in, guided by *spirit* at the heart of creation. "Creation" for him was a bigger word than "universe," especially if there were other universes, as scientists were postulating. So, in spite of the creationists, Peter and Suzanne were sticking with the word in their new book title *Communion and Intercommunion in Creation*, for they were convinced that this was the context necessary for the transformation of shallow secular humanism and divisive religious fundamentalism. Humanity must respond to the deeps of creation in a new way.

When the book came out and received much publicity, an intensity of reaction from the religious right occurred. It had moved beyond radio talk show hyperbole to death threats. From whom? Bible-believing "Christians." Not only did Peter make their phone numbers and addresses more private, they had to go incognito as celebrities had learned to do. The FBI began tracking the threats, and at his speaking engagements police and some agents were keeping an eye out.

What Peter could not begin to make sense of was the hatred their seemingly innocent books and talks elicited. Obviously he was hitting a mythological and cultural nerve. Obviously the fundamentalists' belief in a magical god and his virgin-born incarnate son, who had come to save sinners by his blood, was worth at least the threat of death to unbelievers. It came down to "If you don't agree with my understanding of God, I may have to kill you."

But Peter was figuring out this kind of fundamentalism was beyond belief, finally, or beyond religious and cultural truth. Fundamentalists of all religions were seeking absolute security, which is "whoring after false gods." Yet they obsessively chase after them through scriptural literalism and "their God" – who surely was not Peter's understanding of the God of the Judeo-Christian tradition. Like everyone else, fundamentalists know life is absolutely uncertain, uncontrollable, and threatening to every kind of security. But they hate the way life is and lash out at anyone who defiles their ironclad illusions of reality, such as the afterlife. They're as dangerous as a cornered animal and will do crazy things to defend their false gods. And this was only the 90s. It would get much worse as global terror in the name of Allah would take it to the next level.

As Peter was getting older, life was more fragile for him, especially because his creation-centered ideas were causing a post-modern firestorm. His publisher thought that was great. But more and more it disturbed Peter. How to overcome his liberal bigotry, even his *liberal* fundamentalism? How to bow to the other as a *thou* and to enable the other to bow in return? How to be a reconciler among warring beliefs? How to bow to those who would even persecute me, Peter reflected? He was beginning to understand that Jesus' teaching of love for the enemy was at the heart of spirituality in any day.

New Vision

Peter saw that the Judeo-Christian scriptures were talking about the power of the *spirit* of God and *spirit* of Christ as the presence of the *holy spirit* in any time, from the very beginning to the futuric "omega point." Out of this context he understood and paraphrased the "Prologue" to the Gospel of John (1:1-19):

> In the beginning was *spirit*, the source of authentic being. *Spirit* shines from the heart of creation. Nothing has ever been able to hide its glory.

> A man was called by *spirit* to witness to its power, so that all might understand the profundity of being in creation. He testified to this central fact: *spirit* is in creation but seldom seen, and if seen, seldom becomes one's point of reference.

> However, some have seen and bowed to its transforming power and have been reborn, as it were, conceived by *spirit* – thus its children – even virgin born.

> *Spirit* is always already present among us, the central dynamism of creation, offering

its grace and truth to all beings as sheer gift that never stops giving.

We all can come to know its presence and power through ones who lived at one with and became transparent to *spirit* – if you saw them, you saw *spirit*, eternally present.

And we too, bowing to *spirit*, saying "yes" to *spirit* as it encounters us and we see it, we too become transparent ones, transparent to its presence.

After hearing a speech by the father of deconstructionism, Peter wrote:

That Which Will Not Deconstruct

You call it what you will . . .
    spirit is awe-fully real
    it graciously fulfills
    gives wonder and passion
    it is true and certain
    earning our faith and trust
    it is the greatest loss
    run to it or from it
    all reveals its presence
    all's transparent to it
    all is therefore holy
    spirit permeates all
    consecrates creation
    spirit's primordial

it is never absent
spirit is here for aye

In his journal he wrote:

The Tao [*spirit*] is that from which you cannot depart; if you can depart from it, it's not the Tao [*spirit*]. ~*Confucius*

Where can I go from Thy Spirit? ~*Psalmist*

Spirit is the only thing that is never absent. ~*Wilber*

Spirit's always present (SAP). ~*Peter*

And Peter closed his presentation at an interfaith conference in San Francisco:

I yearn to speak to all spirit traditions in a way that they can sense their commonality rather than their dividedness.

The universal concept of *spirit* is key. Let us think about these four gifts of the *spirit*: *presence*, *grace*, *communion*, and *intercommunion*, which seem in tune with all spirit traditions. These four transforming concepts emphasize the sacred at-one-ment of creation.

As for us humans, passion and zest for living one great life and dying one great death arise out of communion with the *spirit*. Our bliss is being at one with

165

spirit. With such understanding, any religion can be transformed into a conscious unity with creation – including other traditions – rather than trapped in a belief system it must defend as the only truth and the only way. Our best defense is an offense of unity.

The promise is that *spirit* is forever freeing us and setting our feet upon the *spirit* way, the Jesus way, the way of Muhammad, the way of Buddha.

There is a new mood in all this. Instead of a numbing cynicism and an existential cloud, there is the glory of *spirit*'s presence: therefore the smile on the Buddha's face as he saw reality the way it is; therefore Jesus' utterance on the cross, "into thy hands I commend my spirit," as he experienced the awesome power of his always present "Father"; and therefore Muhammad's opening the heart of Aly to receive grace and be transformed. The presence of the *spirit*, with its gifts, brings a new humanness of hope and joy and compassion toward all.

To sum up, the presence and grace of *spirit* and communion with *spirit* generate intercommunion among *spirit's* creation. Humans are given to live on behalf of not only the next generation, or the next seven as the Sioux Indians say, but on behalf of the next thousand years, yea, the next million years; humans are called to live on behalf of the non-human and the human, the smallest and the largest, the nearest and farthest, the most related and the most strange, the friend and the enemy.

I dream that the institutions of the religions of *spirit* see themselves coming from all the past, living on behalf of all the future, at one with all that is now, in profound depth. Such an evolutionary spirituality is what is essential for these times, these places, and all spirit "journers."

Enough of me and mine and ours. Evolution does not primarily have to do with personal human development but with the universal journey of all, in which all are interrelated and unfolding out of the past into the future, eternally at one with *spirit*.

You want fulfillment. Oneness is it. You want significance. Union is it. You want vocation. Unity is it. That which unites is of the *spirit*; that which divides, *not*. All we need to know is "We are one in *spirit*!" So simple. Everyone has sensed this truth. Isn't it time your religion and mine radically and sacrificially embody *spirit's* paradigm of oneness?

But as Peter's spiritual vision heightened he was losing his physical sight – another life-changing event. Several doctors had looked at him but were stupefied by the fast degeneration. The rare disease was affecting the optic nerve in each eye simultaneously. No therapies helped. There appeared to be no way to even slow the process down. They gave Peter a year, two at the most, till he would be considered legally blind.

Suzanne and Adam grieved, and so did he. First, he feared he would not be able to continue reading and writing, but Suzanne promised she would become his eyes to read to him and his fingers to type for him, though he was a good typist. What they couldn't figure out together, somebody from the publishing company would help.

Then he was afraid his quality of life would suffer. He wouldn't be able to drive, to watch the sunset, to see Adam's children if and when they were born, to gaze at his beautiful wife, to go to the movies, to see into the eyes of another in deep communication.

But his deepest fear was whether or not he would live his life "with open eyes and a joyous heart" no matter whatever came, knowing that the situation is never the problem, but one's relationship to the situation can be. Could he face his real situation day after day for years to come? Would he continue to live his life to the full?

He began to set his new world in order.

They bought the biggest computer screen and learned how to magnify the computer with the latest software. They bought a big lighted magnifying lamp to attach to his desk. They tested room light conditions, began to design the room for hand rails and his logical walking patterns, and began to find a specific place for everything he used in the office and the other rooms.

One night, as they lay in bed doing their end-of-day reflection together, each citing three events of the day and naming the day "the great day of _____," Peter told Suzanne, "I feel like Noah preparing for the flood."

She hugged him to her tenderly and said, "We can name our little place Mount Ararat, the high place of peace amidst the storm."

Peter, "You're a poet."

Suzanne, "And you know what they did to give thanks?"

Peter, "Built an altar."

Suzanne, "This bed is the center of the altar of our home."

Peter hugged her and said, "I'm glad you're the high priestess."

They made love. Later, as Peter slept, he dreamed of being safe within a raging storm.

Adam did marry and fathered three children, wondrous to Peter and Suzanne, the adoring grandparents. They were glad he and his loving middle-eastern wife could live in Egypt where Adam was professor of cosmology at the university. But they were sad that they were so far away. They saved air-mile points for a couple of visits a year and were first in line to subscribe to low-cost, broadband international phoning. They stayed in constant contact, sometimes even daily.

Adam was in touch with Thomas and arranged to present a paper in his honor at an earth jurisprudence meeting in China. Thomas had catalyzed global thinking on the rights of all species and would not be satisfied until all national Constitutions became inclusive and not just centered on human rights.

Suzanne, besides being the eyes of Peter, was in the process of having the first book of her own published, entitled *Local Care for the Earth: How to Organize and Motivate Community Groups*. They were a virtual publishing operation in their adjoining offices in their small townhome, where they were learning to be productive individually and together. With the help of the publishing company, Peter hired a part-time secretary to help organize and type for him. Therefore, Suzanne was promoted to general secretary.

Peter's fourth book, just out, was a book of meditations following up on Thomas' latest book about everyone's particular work as part of the great work of helping the earth community move into what he named the "Ecozoic Era" of care for all by all.

Peter was working on his fifth book, his own spirit journey. He wanted to leave a testament to Adam and the grandchildren, to whom he would dedicate his memoir. But more than that, he wanted to tell the story to as many people as possible of his own incredible spirit journey.

Why? Because he felt called to evangelize, to witness to his journey with *spirit,* which was what his whole life was about: following the unfolding journey with *spirit* and watching his life evolve out of a narrow creed of belief into a grand cosmology about the meaning of creation and his existence in it.

He was absolutely sure – if one can be absolutely sure about anything – that at the *heart* of the journey was the life-changing *spirit* that gives grace, through faith, for works of love (yes, even in blindness, or maybe especially in blindness); that the *context* for the journey was the good creation, the sacred journey of the whole universe; and that the *vocation* of the journey was to care for the spirits of all, being about the great work of the human venture on behalf of the earth venture.

As he recalled the hundreds of events of

his life, Peter realized how he was being forcefully changed from his many expressions of group-centeredness, bordering on "bigotry," that is, if one used the definition of being strongly partial to one's group or circle – or even one's culture – and intolerant of those outside. Peter knew that his life-events were forcing him to deal with his major bigotries: being white, American, middle class, educated, clergy, Judeo-Christian, human, and liberal. How he had struggled to turn away from his bigotries was helping him frame the major sections of his story. But more, transcending his bigotries was reminding him of the oneness of creation, that all are one and equal in their diversity. His experiences were relentless in guiding him to the *eternal fact of oneness*, over and over, deeper and deeper.

Also, as he reflected on his myriad life-events, he realized he was writing a psalm of thanksgiving, for he really knew that he had experienced grace upon grace – that his life *was* graced – and, therefore, he could give thanks for his whole journey. Now Peter's passion was to tell readers that creation is full of *grace* and that their lives are guided by *spirit*.

He was writing that all are journers together on the grace-filled spirit journey.

Communicant of
Eternal Creation

On a summer evening, as Peter sat with his one-year-old granddaughter in his lap, with his nine-year-old granddaughter on one side, and his seven-year-old grandson on the other, he listened as they described the stars to him. The one-year-old pointed up and jabbered. Peter reminded them that they all came from stars. Soon the little one crawled down and toddled back into the house. A little later, the older two tiptoed away when Grandfather Peter fell asleep.

***

He dreamed he was conversing with seven other creatures: a gnarled dogwood tree; his mentors Joseph and Thomas; a young Aboriginal girl; a bald eagle; St. Paul; and Mary. An awesome group, each a credit to its species.

Dogwood spoke first, "If there is one thing that demands all our attention, it's that scene there. Just look at it: the red blossoms of the bougainvillea and the palm trees, the woman walking with her dog on the beach, the crashing waves, the dark sky meeting the ocean in the distance – seamlessly – and the setting sun turning the clouds to a rose-red. Here we sit, taking it all in. I cannot imagine a more communal scene. We are all part of one thing, don't you think?"

"And what would you call that one thing?" asked Journer.

"I would call it *Eden*," said the eagle, as he lifted to full height and spread his wings.

Joseph, "I'd call it *Awesome Moment*."

Then Journer asked, "What about you, little one, what would you call that scene?"

The Aboriginal girl did not answer right off. The eagle started to speak, but Journer shushed her with a finger against his lips.

She said in a quiet voice, "It be *Dream-time*."

Thomas, "Yes, the *Dream of the Earth*."

Mary, "I call it *God's Good Creation*."

Joseph, "What would you name it, Journer?"

Journer, "I'd call it *Common Destiny*. We humans are really beginning to care for creation again – as did our ancestors – even as you trees and eagles and aborigines have never stopped doing. All of us are about one thing. We are bound to be about the great work of creation, as Thomas says, or making manifest the other world in this world, as Joseph says.

174

Only within the common destiny of creation are we unique beings, but each with the same purpose. Our history is the history of creation. Our future is the future of creation. We are one."

St. Paul, "Sounds like you're talking about the *Reconciliation of the Cosmos*."

Mary, "What you mean?

St. Paul, "There are two all-determining facts: sin and grace."

Journer, "Or separation and union."

Joseph, "And grace is what triggers the 'union.' I like that word better. Reminds me of a prodigal son returning home. 'Reunion' is even better."

Journer, "All things are united in spite of themselves. We can't gain nor lose union, but we can become aware of it, thankfully."

St. Paul, "Union and reunion all the more abound because of grace. I started my sermons and letters with the salutation of God's grace, telling all hearers that grace belongs to all, all the time."

Journer, "Grace is the bottom-line of the New Testament and Christianity."

Joseph, "Of course. Grace is the bottom-line of creation and existence – of everything."

Thomas, "And as St. Paul writes in several of his letters, there is cosmic union."

Mary, "Like da part where he say creation

175

is standing on tiptoe, yearning to be one."

St. Paul, "I think we all agree that our journey is about growing up into the oneness of creation. But let's be very clear that God in Christ is the crux of this whole enterprise of living at one in creation."

Joseph, "Amen. But let's not give anyone the idea that we have to be Christians to be at one with creation."

Journer, "Let's just say we're all on a journey about bowing to *spirit* at the heart of creation."

St. Paul, "I bow to all in the name of Christ."

Joseph, "I bow to all in the name of grace."

Mary, "I bow to all in da name of Jesus."

Dogwood, "I bow the universe."

Girl, "I bow to all in the name of Wandjina.

Eagle, "I bow to all in the name of seeing."

Thomas, "I bow to the numinous power."

Journer, "I bow to *spirit*."

St. Paul grinned and shouted, "Amen."

The other seven, caught up in the spontaneity of their ritual, shouted back, "Be it so."

And suddenly, without warning, a gale of wind engulfed Journer. Within its vortex he was taken in and lifted up, the newest communicant of eternal creation, at one with all that ever was, is, and ever shall be.

Mary waved her arms, overjoyed. She remembered when she had named him "Journer" and knew then "he be on the great journey without end."

Joseph began a Zorba dance, singing a song he and others had written years before, to the tune of "If I Were a Rich Man," from *Fiddler On the Roof*, sung by Tevye.

In the world of spirit, radically contingent,
*   trustful expectation, intense shock,*
Life's impacted by the mystery and it's all
*   a cloud of awe.*
In the world of spirit, revelation of enigma,
*   wheel of fortune, no excuse;*
One essential task, create the world, sudden reeling,
*   mystery's won the day.*

    Chorus
    Oneness of all creation wholly engulfed
        in marching with all of history,
    Binding the wounds of time,
        everything's worthwhile;
    The other world you see through all and move
        mountains and there's none to show the way,
    All in love with life and all poured out.

In the world of spirit, resurrectional existence,
*   gloriously condemned to waltz;*
Rapture walks with woe, struck dumb by bliss,
*   playing in a symphony.*
In the world of spirit, irresistibly impelled,
*   and simply all atingle now,*

Running on an endless marathon, sudden reeling,
mystery has won the day.

On it went. Mary joined in, hobbling in rhythm.
Dogwood swayed. The girl did a kangaroo hop.
St. Paul and Thomas clapped their hands and
guffawed together. Eagle did small circles of
flight. And they all sang the chorus one more
time.

Journer smiled as he watched and listened
from afar.

***

Peter woke up and just sat there smiling the
deepest smile he'd ever smiled. After feeling
no one on the sofa with him, he picked up his
stick and walked – careful step after careful
step – back into the house. He was singing the
chorus as he entered, imitating Tevye. Peter's
great family laughed and applauded. He
finished and bowed to all.

About the Author

John Cock, a native of southeastern USA, is author/editor of seven books. He is a blogger, retreat guide, and a program facilitator with the Center for Ecozoic Studies, a group inspired by Thomas Berry. He employs the methods of the Order: Ecumenical, a group inspired by Joseph Mathews.

About the Cover Artist

Ellen Howie, of Altamont, NY, describes her cover image: "This mandala is out to invoke a sense after the cosmic sacredness of every moment." She is an artist, a nurse, a spiritual director, and an ICA volunteer.

About the Cover Designer

Tara McDermott is a graphic designer from Dubuque, IA, where she renders art, designs covers and interior art, and provides photo research. She is the mother of two small children, Maggie and Jimmy.